哈福

哈福

哈福

哈福

可以馬上學會的超強英語會/話/課

張瑪麗・Lily Thomas —— 合著

高效練習會話・聽力

哈福

前言 高效練習會話·聽力

◆誰應該閱讀本書？

本書模擬最道地、最實用的美國家庭生活對話，將美式的文化活生生的呈現出來，讓你不但可以學會一口道地的純美語，更可以破除文化上的隔閡，完全的融入英語世界。

適合多方位的英語學習者，不論是初學英語者、英語自學者、學了很久的英語卻説不出口的人、想完全摒棄洋涇浜的人，你們將會發現這是一本徹底增進英語能力的入門好書。

在全球化的影響下，各國商業、金融、文化互相交流日益頻繁，越來越多人基於事業、個人和跟進世界潮流的需求下，必須學好國際的語言—英語。

但是對於英語非母語的人來説，和外國人交談的機會少之又少，更別説了解他們在説什麼，這時候千萬別以為全是英語能力不好的關係，更多時候是文化上的隔閡，就好比説一群愛好高爾夫球的人在談論高爾夫球，對一個完全不懂高爾夫球的人來説，在一旁根本是鴨子聽雷。

◆你可以從本書學到什麼？

所以本書要讓你熟悉美式家庭生活裡，夫妻、親子、家人、朋友、鄰居、一般人之間最常說的美語，從美國人最重視的生活開始，先了解他們的生活方式，再從朋友間的聊天，知道美國人共同的話題是什麼。想要跟進世界潮流就得學習美國人喜歡上圖書館的好習慣；知道如何迅速地找到所需的資料，和大量的閱讀來增廣見聞。

更進一步地進入美國人日常生活的圈子，例如你上美容院、到汽車修理廠、進雜貨店買東西，從這些生活中和各行各業的人交談的內容裡，迅速地掌握他們最基本的生活形態，一方面學習英語，一方面了解道地的美式文化。

書中全部以最簡單、實用的對話，以清晰易讀的方式呈現，讓你一學就會，加上簡易的文法分析，釐清華人最容易混淆的時態問題，還有句型練習、道地美國口語的介紹，讓你可以舉一反三的廣泛應用英語，並不自覺地說出：「美語這麼簡單。」

多聽、多看、多練習是學習美語的必備條件，當然好的教材與正確的美語更是不可或缺的資源，本書絕對讓你脫口說出一口道地的純美語。

Lesson 1

Helen 去度假

Lesson 1 Helen 去度假

MP3 02

實用會話 1

Helen 去度假，在度假的地方打電話給她先生 Patrick

Patrick	Hello, Helen. （哈囉，海倫） How is your trip going? （旅遊好玩嗎？）
Helen	Oh, it's wonderful. （噢，很好。） The islands are beautiful this time of year. （每年的這個時候，島嶼好漂亮。） And the weather is wonderful. （而且氣候很棒。） I wish you and Victoria could have come. （我真希望你和維多利亞也在這裡。）
Patrick	I wish we could have, too. （我也希望我們能去。）

I need a vacation.
（我需要休假。）

When will you be back?
（你什麼時候回來？）

單字

trip [trɪp] 旅程；旅遊	**wish** [wɪʃ] 希望
wonderful [ˈwʌndɚfəl] 好棒的；絕妙的；好極了	**weather** [ˈwɛðɚ] 天氣
island [ˈaɪlənd] 名 島	**vacation** [vəˈkeʃən] 名 休假；假期
beautiful [ˈbjutəfəl] 形 美麗的	**back** [bæk] 回來

實用會話 2

Helen 告訴 Patrick 她飛機回來的時間，並看看他能不能來接機

Helen

My plane lands on Friday at 8:15 a.m.
（我的飛機星期五，八點十五分到。）

Are you still able to pick me up?
（你還是可以來接我嗎？）

Or should I call a taxi when I land?
（還是，我到了之後必須自己叫計程車。）

Patrick

I can still pick you up.
（我還是可以去接你。）

If I get everything finished, we can spend the weekend together.
（如果我事情都做完了，我們可以一起度週末。）

Maybe we can take Victoria to the zoo.
（或許我們可以帶維多利亞去動物園。）

Helen

That sounds like a great idea.
（那聽起來是個好主意。）

I can't wait.
（我真是等不及。）

單字

land [lænd] 動 著陸	**weekend** ['wik'ɛnd] 名 週末
pick someone up 接	**zoo** [zu] 動物園
taxi ['tæksɪ] 計程車	**sound** [saʊnd] 動 聽起來
finish ['fɪnɪʃ] 完成	**idea** [aɪ'dɪə] 主意；概念
spend [spɛnd] 動 花（時間）	**wait** [wet] 等

MP3 03

實用會話 3

Helen 跟 Patrick 說過接機的事情之後，就問起他們的女兒 Victoria

Helen How is Victoria doing, anyhow?
（維多利亞現在怎麼樣？）

Patrick She seems okay but I haven't seen her around much.
（她看起來是還好，但是我也不常看到她。）

	I've been working overtime and she's been studying. （我一直在加班，而她一直在唸書。） Her friend Michael was here earlier. （她的朋友邁克稍早前來過。） They are working really hard on a school report. （他們很認真在做一個學校的報告。） In fact, they're at the library right now. （事實上，他們現在是在圖書館。） They've gone every day this week. （這個星期，他們每天都去。）
Helen	Well, tell her I love her and I'll see her on Friday. （那，告訴她，我愛她，我星期五見她。） I've got to go now. （我該走了。）
Patrick	All right, then. （那，好吧。）

	I'm glad you called. （很高興你打電話來。） You have a good time and be careful. （祝你玩的愉快，也要小心。） I'll see you on Friday morning. （星期五早上見。） I miss you. （我很想你。）
Helen	I miss you, too. （我也很想你。） Bye-bye. （再見。）

單字

anyhow [ˈɛnɪhau] 不管怎麼說；無論如何	**overtime** [ˈovɚˌtaɪm] 加班
seem [sim] 似乎	**earlier** [ˈɝlɪɚ] 形 稍早；較早的；（early 的比較級）

really [ˈriəlɪ] 真的	library [ˈlaɪˌbrɛrɪ] 名 圖書館
hard [hɑrd] 努力的	glad [glæd] 高興
report [rɪˈport] 報告	careful [ˈkɛrfəl] 小心；仔細的
in fact 事實上	miss [mɪs] 動 想念

文法解析

1. 時態：

1.a. 未來式：

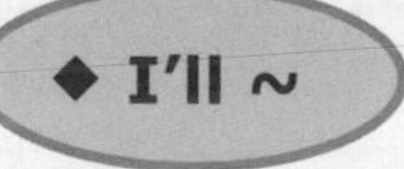

I'll see you on Friday morning.

（我們星期五早上見。）

I'll see her on Friday.

（我星期五要跟她見面。）

I'll give you a call later.

（我稍後再打電話給你。）

I'll tell you how it goes.

（我會告訴你，事情進行得如何。）

◆ When will you ~ ?

When will you be back?

（你什麼時候回來？）

When will you let me know?

（你什麼時候讓我知道？）

When will you get your grades?

（你什麼時候會拿到成績？）

When will you be finished?

（你什麼時候會做好？）

1.b. 過去式

Her friend Michael was here earlier.
（她的朋友邁克稍早在這裡。）

She was angry.
（她剛剛在生氣。）

His mother was sick.
（他的母親病了。）

He was on his way to school when it happened.
（這件事發生時，他正在到學校的路上。）

2. 助動詞

2.a. can

We can spend the weekend together.
（這個週末我們可以在一起。）

Maybe we can take Victoria to the zoo.
（我們或許可以帶維多利亞去動物園。）

We can get together later.
（稍後我們可以在一起聚聚。）

We can go to the movies next week.
（下個星期我們可以去看電影。）

2.b. should

Should I call a taxi when I land?
（我到達之後，應該叫計程車嗎？）

Should I have him call you?
（我應該叫他打電話給你嗎？）

Should we bring anything?
（我們應該帶什麼東西過來？）

Should you eat that?
（那個東西你應該吃嗎？）

3.c. wish ~ could have

I wish you and Victoria could have come.
（我希望你和維多利亞都能來這裡。）

I wish she could have told me sooner.

（我希望她能早一點告訴我。）

I wish John could have known my father.

（我希望約翰能早一點認識我父親。）

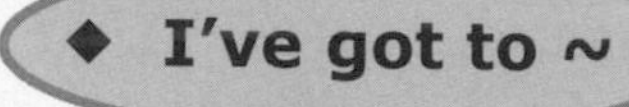

◆ I've got to ~

I've got to take care of that.

（我必須照料那件事。）

I've got to go to the store.

（我必須去商店。）

She's got to get her work done.

（她必須把工作做完。）

He's got to let me know by tomorrow.

（他明天之前必須讓我知道。）

◆ Are you still able to ~

Are you still able to pick me up?

（你還是能夠來接我嗎？）

Are you still able to come?

（你還是能夠來嗎？）

Are Michael and Karen still able to help you?

（邁克和凱倫還是能夠幫你的忙嗎？）

Are those men still able to work?

（那些人還是能夠工作嗎？）

美國口語

That sounds like a good idea.

A: Do you want to go to the movies later?

B: That sounds like a good idea.

A: 你等一下要不要去看電影？

B: 聽起來是個好主意。

◆ I can't wait.

A: Tonight is Patrick's birthday party.

B: I know, I can't wait!

A: 今晚是派崔立克的生日宴會。

B: 我知道，我真是等不急去參加。

成語

◆ take care of

We have an important account I've got to take care of.

（我們有一個重要的客戶我必須負責。）

Did you take care of your problem?

（你的問題解決了嗎？）

That's taken care of.

（那已經解決了。）

He took care of it.

（他把事情解決了。）

Can you take care of the situation?

（這種情況你能解決嗎？）

Lesson 2
好朋友聊天

Lesson 2 好朋友聊天

MP3 05

實用會話 1

Lisa 跟 Karen 是好朋友，這天 Karen 想到好久沒跟 Lisa 聯絡了，所以就打了個電話給 Lisa.

Lisa	Hello. （哈囉。）
Karen	Hello Lisa, it's Karen. （哈囉，莉沙，是我凱倫。）
Lisa	Oh, hi Karen. （噢，嗨，凱倫。） I was just thinking about you. （我剛剛才在想你。） How've you been? （你近來可好？）
Karen	I'm doing pretty well. （很好。） How about yourself? （你自己呢？）
Lisa	I'm doing great. （我很好。）

單字

think[θɪŋk] 想	**yourself** [jʊr'sɛlf] 你自己
pretty ['prɪtɪ] 副 非常；相當	**great** [gret] 很好

實用會話 2

接著 Karen 就問起 Lisa 的先生 Jesse 和他們的孩子們

Karen	How's Jesse and the kids? （傑西和孩子們呢？） I haven't seen them in so long. （我好久沒看到他們了。）
Lisa	They're wonderful. （他們很好。） How's Michael? （你家邁克呢？）
Karen	Oh, he's doing pretty well. （噢，他很好。）

He's still working at the music store.
（他還是在樂器行上班。）

And he's doing well in school.
（他在學校功課也很好。）

單字

kid [kɪd] 小孩子	**work** [wɝk] 工作
wonderful [ˈwʌndɚfəl] 好棒的；絕妙的；好極了	**music** [ˈmjuzɪk] 音樂
still [stɪl] 副 仍然	**store** [stor] 名 商店

實用會話 3

Lisa 也告訴 Karen 她兒子 Miochael 的情形

Lisa I'm glad he can keep his grades up and work.
（我真高興，他能一面上班，還保持好成績。）

You're lucky, Karen.
（凱倫，你真幸運。）

	You've got a good boy. （你有個好兒子。）
Karen	I know. （我知道。） But sometimes I feel bad about his having to work. （但是，必須讓他上班，我有時覺得很過意不去。） And I feel bad about working so much myself. （而且，我自己這麼忙，我也覺得不好。）
Lisa	I wouldn't worry about it. （如果是我，我可不擔心那麼多。） It's not always easy but you are both doing good. （這可不容易，但是，你們兩個都做得很好。）

單字

grade [gred] 成績	**feel** [fil] 感覺
lucky ['lʌkɪ] 形 幸運的	**bad** [bæd] 不好

sometimes ['sʌm'taɪmz] 有時	**both** [boθ] 兩個…（都）
myself [maɪ'sɛlf] 我自己	**always** ['ɔlwez] 總是
worry ['wɝɪ] 動 憂慮	**easy** ['izɪ] 形 容易的

MP3 06

實用會話 4

Lisa 又接著問 Karen 的工作情形

Lisa How is work anyway?
（你的工作怎麼樣？）

Karen We have a new boss, Mr. Thomas.
（我們換了個新老闆，湯姆斯先生。）

He's a lot nicer to work for than the last guy.
（在他手下工作，比上次那個傢伙好多了。）

Lisa I remember Mr. Clark.
（我記得克拉克先生。）

	What a jerk! （真是個討厭鬼。）
Karen	I completely agree. （我完全同意。） But I really like Mr. Thomas a lot. （但是我真的非常喜歡湯姆斯先生。） Well, look, I've got to go. （嗯，我該走了。）

單字

boss [bɔs] 名 主管；老闆	**jerk** [dʒɝk] 惹人討厭的人
guy [gaɪ] （口語）男士	**completely** [kəm'plitlɪ] 完全地
remember [rɪ'mɛmbɚ] 記得	**agree** [ə'gri] 動 同意

實用會話 5

Karen 邀 Lisa 週末一起出去吃午飯

Karen	Are you doing anything this weekend? （你這個週末有空嗎？）
Lisa	I don't really have any plans. （我沒什麼打算。）
Karen	Maybe we should go to lunch on Saturday. （或許我們星期六可以一起去吃個午飯。）
Lisa	Oh that would be fun. （噢，那很好。） I tell you what, I'll call you on Friday to make sure we're still on. （就這麼辦好了，我星期五打電話給你，跟你確認一下。）
Karen	Great, I'll talk to you then. （很好，到時再聊。）

Lisa

Okay, Karen.
（好的，凱倫。）

Thanks for calling.
（謝謝你打電話來。）

It was good talking to you.
（跟你聊天真好。）

Bye.
（再見。）

單字

weekend ['wik'ɛnd] 週末	**fun** [fʌn] 好玩；樂趣
plan [plæn] 計畫	**sure** [ʃʊr] 確定

MP3 07

文法解析

1. 時態

1.a. 未來式

◆ **Are ~**

Are you doing anything this weekend?

（你這個週末有什麼事嗎？）

Are you going to the concert?

（你要去參加演唱會嗎？）

Are you moving next month?

（你下個月要搬家嗎？）

Are you coming over?

（你要過來嗎？）

1b. 現在式（一件事實）

◆ **Have**

We have a new boss.

（我們換了個新老闆。）

They have eight cats.
（他們有八隻貓。）

I have an old car.
（我有一部舊車。）

We have a blue house.
（我有一間藍色的房子。）

1c. haven't + 過去分詞 (現在完成式)

I haven't seen them.
（我一直都沒看到他們。）

They haven't told me.
（他們還沒有告訴我。）

We haven't decided.
（我們還沒決定。）

2. 助動詞

2a. wouldn’t

I wouldn’t worry about it.

（是我，我可不擔心那個。）

I wouldn’t feel bad.

（是我，我可不覺得難過。）

He wouldn’t care about that.

（他不會關心的。）

She wouldn’t try.

（她不會試的。）

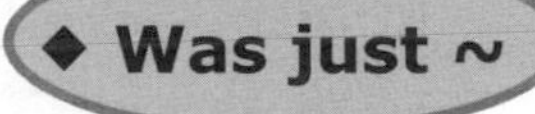

◆ Was just ~

I was just thinking about you.

（我剛剛才在想你。）

It was just talking to her.

（我剛剛才在跟她說話。）

She was just telling me that.

（她剛剛才在跟我說那件事。）

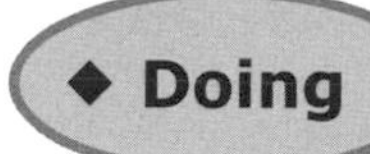

◆ Doing

I'm doing pretty well.

（我很好。）

She's doing great.

（她做得很好。）

He's doing fine.

（他做的還好。）

Michael's doing well.

（邁克做得很好。）

美國口語

◆ You're lucky!

A: I am going on vacation this weekend.

B: You're lucky!

A: 這個週末我要去度假。

B: 你真幸運。

◆ What a jerk!

A: Can you believe he didn't even call me?

B: What a jerk!

A: 你相信嗎，他竟然沒有打電話給我？

B: 真是個討厭鬼。

Lesson 3

Michael上圖書館

Lesson 3

Michael 上圖書館

MP3 08

實用會話 1

Michael 在圖書館跟圖書管理員 Mrs. Carter 聊天

Mrs. Carter	Hello there, Michael. （邁克，你好。）
Michael	Hi, Mrs. Carter. （嗨，卡特太太。） I wanted to say thanks for helping me with my report. （我要謝謝你幫忙我的報告。） The book you recommended was very useful. （你介紹的書本很有用。）
Mrs. Carter	Good, I'm glad it was helpful. （很好，我很高興，那本書幫的上忙。） How'd that report go after all? （你的報告結果如何呢？）

Michael	Well, I haven't got my grade yet but I think it went well. （嗯，我還沒拿到報告的成績，但是我想應該是做得很好。）
Mrs. Carter	I'm glad to hear that. （我很高興聽到你這麼說。） I know how hard you worked on it. （我知道你很用心做那份報告。）

單字

report [rɪ'port] 報告	**helpful** ['hɛlpfəl] 形 有幫助的
recommend [ˌrɛkə'mɛnd] 推薦；介紹	**after all** 究竟
useful ['jusfəl] 有用的；有助益的	**grade** [gred] 成績

實用會話 2

圖書管理員 Mrs. Carter 問 Michael 今天來圖書館找什麼書？

Mrs. Carter

So, what are you looking for today?
（那，你今天在找什麼呢？）

Michael

Actually I'm looking for two things.
（事實上，我在找兩樣東西。）

First, I want a good horror story to read.
（首先，我想找一本好的恐怖小說來看。）

Or maybe a mystery.
（或者是懸疑小說也可以。）

Something fun.
（只要是有趣的。）

Mrs. Carter

How about some Edgar Allen Poe or a Sherlock Holmes mystery?
（愛倫波或是福爾摩斯的懸疑小說怎麼樣？）

We've got both of those over in the fiction section.
（我們這兩種書都有，就在小說類的架子上。）

Michael	Great. （很好。） I'll have to check them out. （我可得去看看。） But I also need something for school. （但是，我還要一些學校裡需要的東西。）
Mrs. Carter	Anything I can help you with? （有什麼我可以幫得上忙的嗎？）
Michael	Victoria and I are doing a report on mummies. （維多利亞和我要做有關『木乃伊』的報告。） But we want to do something new. （但是，我們想寫一些新一點的東西。）

單字

horror ['hɔrɚ] 恐怖	**fiction** ['fɪkʃən] 名 小說
story ['storɪ] 故事	**section** ['sɛkʃən] （零售店的）部門；區域
mystery ['mɪstərɪ] 名 神秘；懸疑	**mummies** ['mʌmɪz] 木乃伊（mummy 的複數）

MP3 09

實用會話 3

圖書管理員 Mrs. Carter 介紹一些資料給 Michael 寫報告用

Mrs. Carter

I think I've got just the thing.
（我想，我正好有這些資料。）

Have you ever heard of the Bog People?
（你有沒有聽說過『波格人』？）

They are mummies found in England, I believe.
（我相信，他們是在英國發現的木乃伊。）

We have a book all about them and it has pictures.
（我們有一本書專門在寫他們，而且有照片。）

Michael

Wow, that sounds interesting.
（哇，那聽起來很有趣。）

I'd like to see them.
（我想看看。）

Mrs. Carter

Well, here comes Victoria now.
（嗯，維多利亞來了。）

I'll show you both to find those books.
（我帶你們兩個去找那些書。）

單字

believe [bɪ'liv] 動 相信	**interesting** ['ɪntrɪstɪŋ] 有趣的
picture ['pɪktʃɚ] 圖畫；相片	**show** [ʃo] 展示；帶領
sound [saʊnd] 動 聽起來	**find** [faɪnd] 找到

文法解析

1. 時態

1.a. 現在式

I'm glad to hear that.

（我很高興聽到你這麼說。）

I'm sorry you're hurt.

（你受傷了，我很難過。）

I'm tired.

（我累了。）

I'm sleepy.

（我很睏。）

1.b. 現在式

I want a good horror story.

（我想要一本好的恐怖小說。）

We want to do something new.

（我想要做一些新的事情。）

They want to go swimming.

他們要去游泳。

I want to take a nap.

（我要小睡一下。）

2. 助動詞

2.a. I'd like

I'd like to see them.

（我想要見他們。）

I'd like to go.

（我想要去。）

I'd like to say something.

（我想要說一些話。）

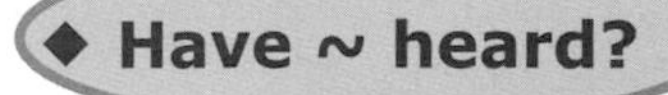

◆ Have ~ heard?

Have you ever heard of the bog people?

（你有沒有聽說過『波格人』？）

Have they ever heard of him?

（他們有沒有聽說過他？）

Havc you ever heard anything so funny?

（你有沒有聽過這麼有趣的事？）

Have you ever heard that saying before?

（你以前有沒有聽說過那個說法？）

◆ We've got ~

We've got both of those.

（那兩個我們都有。）

We've got more than enough.

（我們有夠多的。）

We've got way too much.

（我們有太多了。）

美國口語

◆ I've got just the thing.

A: I need something to get rid of my headache.

B: I've got just the thing.

A: 我需要什麼東西來治我的頭痛。

B: 我有治你頭痛的東西。

◆ I'll show you.

A: I'm not sure how to do this.

B: Here, I'll show you.

A: 我不知道該怎麼做。

B 來，我做給你看。

◆ I'll have to check them out.

A: I saw two dresses you might be interested in.

B: Really? I'll have to check them out.

A: 我看見兩件洋裝，你可能會有興趣。

B: 真的？我一定要去看看。

Memo

Lesson 4

在美容院

Lesson 4 在美容院

MP3 11

實用會話 1

Helen 度假回來，來到她常去的美容院找她的美髮師 May

Miss May	Helen, you look great! （海倫，你好漂亮。）
Helen	Thanks, May. （謝謝你，梅。） So do you. （你也是。）
May	So, how was your trip? （那，你的旅遊好玩嗎？） Tell me all about it. （把你這次的旅遊說給我聽。） Where did you go? （你去哪裡？）
Helen	Well, let's see. （嗯，我來告訴你。）

	I went to the Bahamas. （我去巴哈馬群島。）
May	Did you, really? （真的？） I've always wanted to go to the Bahamas. （我一直都想去巴哈馬群島。） Did you go scuba diving? （你有沒有潛水？）
Helen	Yes, I did and it was great. （有，潛水好棒。） You would not believe how beautiful it was. （你絕不相信有多漂亮。） The whole trip was wonderful. （整趟旅行都很棒。）
May	You are so lucky. （你真幸運。）

I've never gone before.
（我從沒去過。）

Helen Neither had I.
（我也沒去過。）

This was my first time and I loved it.
（這是我第一次去，我真的很喜歡。）

You've definitely got to go sometime.
（你有空一定得去。）

單字

trip [trɪp] 旅程；旅遊	**beautiful** [ˈbjutəfəl] 形 美麗的；漂亮的
always [ˈɔlwez] 總是	**whole** [hol] 全部的；整體的
scuba diving 潛水	**wonderful** [ˈwʌndɚfəl] 好棒的；絕妙的；好極了
believe [bɪˈliv] 動 相信	**lucky** [ˈlʌkɪ] 形 幸運的

before [bɪ'for] 之前	**definitely** ['dɛfənətlɪ] 確定地；肯定地
first [fɝst] 第一次	**sometime** ['sʌmtaɪm] 哪一天；將來某個時候

實用會話 2

聊天中 Helen 想起來，她去度假時買了紀念品要送給 May

Helen	Oh, that reminds me. （噢，我想起來了。） I brought you something. （我買了東西要送你。）
May	Oh, how sweet! （噢，你真周到。） You shouldn't have! （你實在不用這麼客氣。）
Helen	No, I wanted to. （不，我想這麼做。）

Do you like it?
（你喜歡嗎？）

May I love it!
（我喜歡。）

It's one of the most unusual rings I've ever seen.
（這是我所看過最特別的戒指之一。）

Helen It's made completely out of shell.
（這個完全是用貝殼做的。）

I thought of you when I saw it.
（當我看到它時，就想到你。）

May Thank you so much.
（多謝。）

Helen Don't worry about it.
（別管這個。）

單字

remind [rɪ'maɪnd] 提醒	**ring** [rɪŋ] 戒指
brought [brɔt] 動 帶來； （bring 的過去式，過去分詞）	**ever** ['ɛvɚ] 副 曾經
sweet [swit] 甜的；可愛的	**completely** [kəm'plitlɪ] 完全地
unusual [ʌn'juʒʊəl] 不尋常的	**shell** [ʃɛl] 貝殼

MP3 12

實用會話 3

Helen 把話轉到正題，她要 May 整理一下她的頭髮

Helen

Instead, worry about my hair.
（倒是我的頭髮。）

Look at it!
（你看看。）

It's such a mess from all the water and the sand.
（被水和沙搞成這個樣子。）

Can you fix it up or maybe give me a trim?

（你有辦法整理一下，還是修剪一下嗎？）

I've got a dinner party to go to and I'm a mess.

（我要去參加一個晚宴，而我是亂七八糟的。）

May

I don't think you're a mess at all.

（我不認為你是亂七八糟的。）

But I've got a couple of ideas about how to fix your hair.

（但是，我有一些可以整理你的頭髮的主意。）

Come on and we'll see what we can do.

（來吧，我們來看看怎麼整理你的頭髮好。）

單字

worry ['wɝɪ] 動 憂慮；擔心	**sand** [sænd] 名 沙
hair [hɛr] 頭髮	**fix** [fɪks] 整理
mess [mɛs] 亂七八糟；一團糟	**trim** [trɪm] 動 修剪

party ['pɑrtɪ] 宴會；派對	**idea** [aɪ'dɪə] 主意

MP3 13

文法解析

1. 時態

1.a. 過去式

◆ Went

I went to the Bahamas.
（我去了巴哈馬群島。）

Lisa went to the store.
（莉沙到商店去。）

They went to the movies.
（他們去看電影。）

Victoria went to school.
（維多利亞去上學。）

1.b. 未來式

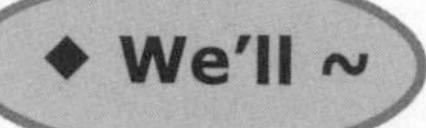

We'll see what we can do.

（我們來看看有什麼辦法。）

We'll try our best.

（我們會盡力。）

We'll be there.

（我們會去。）

We'll let you know.

（我們會讓你知道。）

2. 命令句

2.a. 肯定句

Look at it!　（看看它。）

Fix this.　（把它修理好。）

Help me.　（幫助我。）

Hurry up.　（快一點。）

2.b. 否定句

Don’t worry. （別擔心。）

Don’t cut it. （別剪。）

Don’t fall. （別跌到了。）

Don’t hurt yourself. （別傷到你自己。）

句型練習

◆ I’ve always ~

I’ve always wanted to go to the Bahamas.
（我一直都想去巴哈馬群島。）

I’ve always loved that color.
（我一直都很喜歡那個顏色。）

I’ve always wished for one of these.
（我一直都想要有一樣那些東西。）

◆ You would not believe ~

You would not believe how rude he was.

（你絕不會相信他有多無禮。）

You would not believe what a good deal I got.

（你不會相信我拿到什麼樣的好交易。）

You would not believe the price of stocks.

（你不會相信現在的股價。）

You would not believe what she said.

（你不會相信她說了甚麼話。）

◆ I've never ~

I've never gone before.

（我從沒去過。）

I've never seen one of those.

（那些東西我從沒見過任何一樣。）

I've never played this game.

（我沒玩過這個遊戲。）

I've never eaten German food.

（我沒吃過德國菜。）

美國口語

◆ How sweet!

A: I'm taking my wife out to dinner tonight.

B: How sweet!

A: 我今晚要帶我太太出去吃飯。

B: 你真體貼。

◆ You shouldn't have!

A: I got you a little something today.

B: Really? You shouldn't have!

A: 我今天買了一點小東西要給你。

B: 真的？你不用這麼做的。

◆ I love it!

A: What do you think of my new hairstyle?

B: I love it!

A: 你看我的新髮型怎麼樣？

B: 我很喜歡。

Memo

Lesson 5

在汽車維修廠

Lesson 5 在汽車維修場

MP3 14

實用會話 1

Patrick 把車子拿到汽車維護廠，找技工 Bobby

Bobby	Hello Mr. James. （哈囉，詹姆斯先生。） What can I do for you today? （你今天有什麼事嗎？）
Patrick	Hey there, Bobby. （嗨，巴比。） I'm going to need an oil change. （我的車子需要換機油。）
Bobby	Are you going on a trip? （你要出遠門嗎？）
Patrick	Actually, I am. （是的。） I'm hoping to take my family to the caverns this weekend. （這個週末我希望帶我的家人去洞穴。）

Victoria has always loved to go there.
（維多利亞一直想去。）

Even as a child she loved them and the zoo.
（她很小的時候，就喜歡洞穴和動物園。）

Bobby That sounds like fun.
（聽起來很有趣。）

Especially since you work all the time.
（特別是，你總是在工作。）

Patrick Yeah, I could use a break.
（是的，我需要休息一下。）

單字

actually [ˈæktʃʊəlɪ] 副 實際上；事實上	**zoo** [zu] 動物園
cavern [ˈkævɚn] 洞穴	**especially** [əˈspɛʃəlɪ] 特別是
even [ˈivən] 甚至	**break** [brek] 名 短暫的休息

實用會話 2

Patrick 把話題轉到買賣股票上

Patrick

My stocks are driving me crazy.
（我的股票讓我快瘋了。）

Weren't you interested in the stock market, Bobby?
（巴比，你以前不是對股票很興趣嗎？）

Bobby

Yes, and I still am.
（是的，我還是有興趣。）

But I haven't invested anything yet.
（但是我還沒投資過。）

I've only got a little bit of money saved up.
（我只存了一點錢。）

I don't make that much and I'm still in school.
（我賺的錢不多，而且我還是個學生。）

Patrick	That's true but it doesn't hurt to start looking around. （那倒是真的，但是開始留意也無妨。） You may find a stock that will allow you to make a small investment. （你可能會找到只需要很少錢投資的股票。）
Bobby	To tell you the truth, I don't know much about the market. （說實話，股票市場我是不太懂。）

單字

stock [stɑk] 股票	**invest** [ɪnˈvɛst] 投資
crazy [ˈkrezɪ] 形 瘋狂的	**save** [sev] 節省
market [ˈmɑrkɪt] 市場	**true** [tru] 真的
still [stɪl] 副 仍然	**start** [stɑrt] 開始

單字

hurt [hɝt] 傷害	**investment** [ɪnˈvɛstmənt] 投資
allow [əˈlaʊ] 動 允許	**truth** [truθ] 實話

MP3 15

實用會話 3

Patrick 想幫 Bobby 瞭解股市

Patrick	Well, it's not that hard. （嗯，那不是那麼難。） If you're interested, I could ask my broker to meet with you. （如果你有興趣，我可以叫我的經紀人跟你見見。） He may be able to give you some advice. （他可能可以給你一些建議。）
Bobby	That'd be great.（那可真好。） I'd really appreciate it.（我很感激。）
Patrick	Good.（好。） I'll have Alex give you a call. （我會叫艾力克斯打電話給你。）

單字

hard [hɑrd] 困難的	**advice** [əd'vaɪs] 建議
broker ['brokɚ] 股票經紀人	**appreciate** [ə'priʃɪ,et] 動 感激
meet [mit] 見面	

文法解析

1. 時態

1a. 現在式（否定句）

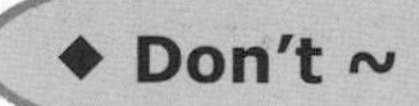

I don't make that much.
（我賺不多。）

You don't need help.
（你不需要幫忙。）

I don't know much.
（我不是知道很多。）

They don't know about it.
（他們不知道。）

2. 助動詞

2.a. may

He may be able to give you some advice.
（他或許可以給你一些建議。）

She may be able to help you.
（她或許可以幫你的忙。）

Jesse may come later.
（傑西稍後或許會來。）

Helen may go to France next week.
（海倫下星期可能會去法國。）

句型練習

◆ Weren't you ~

Weren't you interested in the stock market?

（你不是對股票市場有興趣？）

Weren't you going to the show?

（你不是要去看表演？）

Weren't you mad at him?

（你不是在生他的氣？）

◆ It doesn't hurt ~

It doesn't hurt to start looking around.

（開始留意也無妨。）

It doesn't hurt to plan ahead.

（先計畫也無妨。）

It doesn't hurt to ask.

（問問也無妨。）

It doesn't hurt to save money now.

（存些錢也無妨。）

◆ Give ~ a call

I'll have Alex give you a call.

（我會叫艾力克斯打電話給你。）

Give me a call later.

（稍後打個電話給我。）

Why don't you give him a call?

（你何不打個電話給他？）

Tell Lisa to give Karen a call.

（叫莉沙給凱倫打個電話。）

Memo

美國口語

◆ To tell you the truth ~

A: Eric called you.

B: To tell you the truth, I don't care.

A: 艾力克打電話給你。

B: 老實跟你說，我不在乎。

◆ It's not that hard ~

A: I can't seem to write this paper.

B: It's not that hard once you get started.

A: 我這篇報告好像寫不出來。

B: 你一旦開始，就不那麼難。

Memo

Lesson 6

去雜貨店

Lesson 6 去雜貨店

實用會話 1

MP3 17

Lisa 到雜貨店去買東西，雜貨店的老闆是伍德先生，他看到 Lisa，就跟她打招呼

Mr. Woods Hello there, Lisa.
（哈囉，莉沙。）

Lisa Oh, hello Mr. Woods.
（噢，哈囉，伍德先生。）

Mr. Woods Is there anything I can help you with today?
（有什麼需要我幫忙的地方嗎？）

Lisa Actually, there is.
（確實是有的。）

Do you have any plums?
（你有沒有李子？）

Mr. Woods You're in luck, I sure do.
（你很幸運，我今天有李子。）

And, they're on sale today, only $.99 a pound.
（而且是在打折拍賣，一磅只要九毛九美金。）

Lisa Great!
（很好。）

I'll take three pounds.
（我要三磅。）

Mr. Woods Mary will weigh them for you.
（瑪麗會秤給你。）

單字

anything [ˈɛnɪθɪŋ] 副 實際上；事實上	**on sale** 拍賣
actually [ˈæktʃʊəlɪ] 副 實際上；事實上	**pound** [paʊnd] 磅
plum [plʌm] 李子	**weigh** [we] 動 秤重量

實用會話 2

伍德先生把李子拿給他太太瑪麗，瑪麗正在為客人算帳

Mrs. Woods	How are you doing today, Lisa? （莉沙，你今天好嗎？）
Lisa	I'm doing great. （很好。） How about you? （你呢？）
Mrs. Woods	I'm doing just fine. （我還好。） Thank you for asking. （謝謝你問候。）

實用會話 3

雜貨店老闆娘 Mary 順便問候 Lisa 的孩子們

Mrs. Woods	How are the little ones? （孩子們好嗎？）

Lisa	They're doing great. （他們都很好。） Brandon's getting big and Jennifer just started kindergarten. （布藍登長得越來越高，珍妮佛剛上幼稚園。）
Mrs. Woods	So, that's why I haven't seen them. （那就是我一直沒看到他們的原因。） They've been in school. （他們一直在學校裡。）

單 字

little ['lɪtl̩] 形 小的	**kindergarten** ['kɪndɚgartn̩] 幼稚園
start [stɑrt] 開始	**why** [hwaɪ] 為什麼

MP3 18

實用會話 4

雜貨店老闆娘 Mary 又轉話題問候 Lisa 的先生 Jesse

Mrs. Woods	How's your husband? （你先生好嗎？）

Lisa　Jesse's been working very hard.
（傑西一直都很努力工作。）

But he's doing good.
（但是，他做得很好）。

Mrs. Woods　That's great to hear.
（我很高興聽到這個消息。）

He sure does love these plums, doesn't he?
（他真的很喜歡李子，不是嗎？）

Lisa　Yeah, they're his favorite.
（是啊，李子是他最喜歡的水果。）

I'm thinking about making them into a pie.
（我在想用他們來做水果派。）

Mrs. Woods　Oh, I think he'd like that a lot.
（噢，我想他會很喜歡。）

I may even have a recipe you can use.
（我可能有個食譜你可以用。）

Lisa

That would be great.
（那可真好。）

I'd really appreciate it.
（我很感激。）

Let me know if you come across a good one.
（如果你找到好的食譜，跟我說一聲。）

單字

husband [ˈhʌzbənd] 丈夫	**pie** [paɪ] （水果）派
hard [hɑrd] 努力的	**recipe** [ˈrɛsəpɪ] 食譜
hear [hɪr] 聽到	**appreciate** [əˈpriʃɪˌet] 動 感激
favorite [ˈfevərɪt] 最喜歡的	**come across** 偶然遇見

實用會話 5

雜貨店的老闆伍德先生把 Lisa 要的雜貨和李子一起算好了帳，放在袋子裡，交給 Lisa

Mr. Woods	Well, here you go. （嗯，你買的東西在這裡。） Your total is $15.75. （總共是十五塊七毛五。）
Lisa	Here you are. （錢在這裡。）
Mr. Woods	Thanks, Lisa. （謝謝你。） You have a nice day, now. （祝你一天愉快。） And say hello to Jesse for me. （替我跟傑西問好。）
Lisa	Will do, Mr. Woods. （我會的，伍德先生。）

單字

total ['totl̩]	nice [naɪs]
總共	很好

文法解析

1. 時態

1.a. 未來式

Mary will weigh them for you.
（瑪麗會秤給你。）

I will see you tomorrow.
（我們明天見。）

She will come over later.
（她稍後會來。）

Jesse will be home late tonight.
（今晚傑西會晚一點回來。）

1.b. 現在進行式

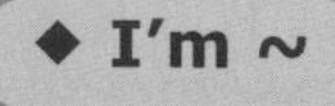

I'm eating breakfast.

（我現在在吃早餐。）

I'm studying for my exam.

（我現在在準備考試。）

I'm reading a book.

（我在看書。）

I'm counting my money.

（我在數我的錢。）

1.c. 現在完成式

◆ Have been

I've been very busy.

（我一直很忙。）

You've been late all week.

（你一整個星期都遲到。）

They've been on sale.

（他們一直在打折拍賣。）

2. 助動詞

2a. can

Is there anything I can help you with today?

（今天有什麼我可以幫忙的嗎？）

Is there anything I can do to help?

（有什麼我可以幫忙的嗎？）

Is there anything I can say to change your mind?

（我可以說什麼才能讓你改變主意？）

Is there anything I can get for you?

（你要我拿什麼東西給你？）

2b. may

I may even have a recipe you can use.

（我可能有個食譜你可以用。）

I may want to stop by later.

（我稍後可能會過來你那邊坐一下。）

He may need you to help him.

（他可能需要你幫他的忙。）

She may call us tonight.

（她今晚可能會打電話給我們。）

句型練習

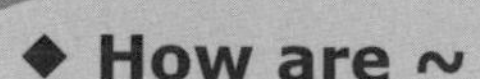

◆ How are ~

How are you doing today, Lisa?

（莉沙，你今天好嗎？）

How are the little ones?

（孩子們好嗎？）

How are your parents?

（你的父母好嗎？）

◆ ~ getting + 形容詞

Brandon's getting big.

（布藍登長的越來越高。）

My dog's getting mean.

（我的狗越來越瘦。）

She's getting sleepy.

（她睏了。）

I'm getting hungry.

（我餓了。）

◆ So that's why.

A: Did you hear that Michael's really sick?

B: So that's why he didn't come to my party.

A: 你有沒有聽說邁克病得很厲害？

B: 原來那是他沒來參加我宴會的原因。

A: You left your book at my house last night.

B: So that's why I couldn't find it.
Thanks for bringing it back to me.

A: 昨晚你把你的書本留在我家。

B: 原來那就是我找不到我的書的原因。
謝謝你拿來給我。

◆ A good one

A: Have you ever read that book, Harry Potter?

B: Oh, that's a good one.
You'll really enjoy it.

A: 你有沒有看過『哈利波特』這本書？

B: 噢，那本書很好看。
你會喜歡的。

A: Did Michael tell you that story about his dog?

B: Yes, that's a good one.

I've never laughed so hard in my life.

A: 邁克有沒有跟你說他的狗的事？

B: 說了，真是有趣。

我這一生還沒笑得那麼厲害過。

◆ Will do.

A: Let me know what the doctor says.

B: Will do.

A: 讓我知道醫生怎麼說。

B: 我會的。

A: Can you pick me up later?

B: Will do.

I'll see you at 7:00.

A: 你稍後可以來接我嗎？

B: 好的。

咱們七點見。

Lesson 7

玩遊戲

Lesson 7 玩遊戲

實用會話 1

MP3 20

Brandon 和他的朋友湯姆在玩球，Brandon 的小妹妹 Jennifer 想跟他們一起完

Jennifer	What are you doing? （你們在做什麼？）
Tom	We're playing ball. （我們在玩球。）
Jennifer	Can I play, too? （我也可以玩嗎？）
Brandon	No. （不行。）
Jennifer	But I want to play. （但是，我要玩。）
Brandon	We just played with you, Jennifer. （我們剛剛跟你玩過了。） Now it's our turn. （現在換我們玩了。）

Jennifer	But I want to play with you. （但是，我要跟你們玩。）
Brandon	Maybe next time, okay. （或許下次吧。） We want to play by ourselves this time. （這一次，我們要自己玩。）

單字

ourselves [aʊr'sɛlvz] 我們自己	**next** [nɛkst] 下一個
play [ple] 動 打球；遊玩	**turn** [tɝn] 輪流
maybe ['mebi] 也許	**time** [taɪm] 次

實用會話 2

布藍登和他的朋友 Tom 不讓 Jennifer 一起玩，Jennifer 就告狀到他們媽媽 Lisa 那裡去

Jennifer

Mom!
（媽。）

Brandon won't let me play!
（布藍登不讓我玩。）

Lisa

How come Jennifer can't play with you guys?
（珍妮佛為什麼不能跟你們玩？）

I don't think it would hurt you to let her play.
（我不認為讓她跟你們玩有什麼不好。）

Brandon

Mom, we just played with her.
（媽，我們剛剛跟她玩過了。）

We want to play ball by ourselves now.
（現在我們要自己玩球。）

Please tell her to leave us alone.
（請告訴她，不要來吵我們。）

Lisa	Will you let her play for just a few minutes, please? （你們讓她玩一下子好嗎？） Then I'll take her in the house. （然後，我就會帶她進屋子來。） She just wants to be with you, Brandon. （布藍登，她只是想跟你一起玩。）
Brandon	Okay, I guess. （好吧。） But just for a few minutes. （但是只玩幾分鐘。）
Lisa	Thanks, Brandon, you're a good boy. （謝謝你，布藍登，你是個好男孩。） Thank you, too, Tom. （也謝謝你，湯姆。）

單字

hurt [hɝt] 傷害	**leave someone alone** 某人 alone 不要去惹某人
leave [liv] 留著	**minute** [ˈmɪnɪt] 名 （時間單位）分
alone [əˈlon] 形 孤單的；單獨的；獨自	**guess** [gɛs] 猜想

實用會話 3

MP3 21

Lisa 說服 Brandon 和 Tom 讓 Jennifer 玩一會兒，現在她要來跟 Jennifer 講清楚，玩一會兒之後，Jennifer 就得跟媽媽進屋去

Lisa Now Jennifer, they're going to play ball with you.
（珍妮佛，現在他們要跟你玩了。）

But then you and me will go inside.
（但是，稍後，你就要跟我進屋子裡去。）

Jennifer But mom, I want to play with Brandon and Tom.
（但是，媽，我想跟布藍登和湯姆一起玩。）

Lisa

I know you do.
（我知道你想要。）

They're going to let you play.
（他們要讓你玩。）

But then we have to let them play.
（但是，稍後，我們一定要讓他們玩。）

One day you'll want to be with your friends without Brandon there.
（有一天，你會希望跟你的朋友玩，而不希望布藍登在旁邊。）

Jennifer

But I want to play.
（但是，我想玩。）

Lisa

Well, we can play.
（那，我可以跟你玩。）

If you want, I'll read you a story or we can play dolls.
（如果你要的話，我可以說故事給你聽，或是我們可以玩娃娃。）

You get to pick whatever you want.
（你可以選擇你要玩什麼。）

Jennifer

Okay, fine.
（好吧。）

單字

play [ple] 打球；玩	**read** [rid] 讀
then [ðɛn] 然後	**story** [ˈstorɪ] 故事
inside [ˈɪnˈsaɪd] 屋裡	**doll** [dɑl] 娃娃
let [lɛt] 讓	**pick** [pɪk] 挑選
friend [frɛnd] 朋友	**whatever** [hwɑtˈɛvɚ] 任何…的事物
without [wɪðˈaʊt] 沒有	**fine** [faɪn] 好吧

MP3 22

文法解析

1. 時態

1.a. 現在進行式

◆ We're ~

We're playing ball.

（我們在玩球。）

We're doing our homework.

（我們在做功課。）

We're eating lunch.

（我們在吃午飯。）

We're making cookies.

（我們在做小餅乾。）

1.b. 過去式

We just played with you, Mary.

（瑪麗，我們才剛跟你玩過。）

They got up late this morning.

（他們今早晚一點起床。）

He went to the store.

（他到商店去。）

I bought a new dress.

（我買了一件新的洋裝。）

1.c. 未來式

◆ You'll ~

You'll like the movie.

（你會喜歡這部電影。）

You'll do better next time.

（下次你會做得更好。）

You'll see.

（你就會知道。）

句型練習

◆ Maybe. . .

Maybe next time.

（或許下次吧。）

Maybe you can play later.

（稍等一下你或許可以玩。）

Maybe they will come over.

（或許他們會過來。）

Maybe I will go to Europe instead.

（或許我會改去歐洲。）

◆ Won't

Brandon won't let me play!

（布藍登不讓我玩。）

Ms. Lee won't accept late papers.

（李老師不收遲交的報告。）

I won't be here tomorrow.
（我明天不會在這裡。）

Dad won't let me go.
（爸爸不讓我去。）

◆ I guess.

A: Jesse, can you pick the kids up after school?
B: Sure, I guess.

A: 傑西，放學後你可不可以去接小孩？
B: 好的。

◆ If you want. . .

A: I'm so bored today.
B: If you want, we can go to a movie.

A: 我今天覺得很無聊。
B: 如果你要的話，我們可以去看電影。

A: Do you want to play dolls?

B: If you want.

A: Okay then, I'll go get them.

A: 你要不要玩娃娃？

B: 如果你要玩的話。

A: 好，那我去拿娃娃。

Memo

Lesson 8
準備去上班上學

Lesson 8 準備去上班上學

實用會話 1

MP3 23

早上，Michael 正要去上學，而他媽媽 Karen 也準備好要去上班

Karen	Good morning, Michael. （早安，邁克。）
Michael	Good morning, mom. （嗎，早安。）
Karen	Did you sleep well? （你昨晚睡的好嗎？）
Michael	Not really. （沒睡好。）
	I was up most of the night doing my report. （我幾乎整晚沒睡，在做我的報告。）
Karen	Did you get it done? （你做完了嗎？）
Michael	Yeah, I finally finished it. （是，終於做完了。）

Karen

I know it's hard working and going to school but hang in there.
（我知道，要工作，又要上學很辛苦，但是別氣餒。）

I'm really proud of you.
（我真的很以你為傲。）

And I know you'll do fine.
（我知道你會做得很好。）

Michael

Thanks, mom.
（媽，謝謝你。）

單字

sleep [slip] 動 睡覺	**finish** [ˈfɪnɪʃ] 完成
well [wɛl] 副 好；適當地	**hard** [hɑrd] 困難的
report [rɪˈport] 報告	**hang in there** 堅持下去
finally [ˈfaɪnḷɪ] 最終；終於	**proud** [praʊd] 感到驕傲

實用會話 2

Karen 問 Michael 今晚是不是還要上班

Karen	So, do you have work again today? （你今天還要工作嗎？）
Michael	Yes, and it's going to be very busy. （是，而且今天會很忙。） We're having a sale but we're going to close early. （我們的東西在打折拍賣，但是我們會提早打烊。） So I should get off around 7:00 tonight. （所以，我今晚會在七點左右下班。） But I've got to go to the library. （但是，我必須到圖書館去。） So I won't actually get home until after 9:00. （所以我九點以後才會回來。）
Karen	Well, I have to work late again, anyway. （嗯，反正，我也會工作到很晚。）

But I should be home by then.
（但是，那個時候我也應該到家了。）

Do you want to order a pizza for dinner?
（你要不要叫比薩餅做晚餐？）

Michael That sounds good.
（好的。）

Karen I'll see you tonight.
（我們晚上見。）

Michael Bye, mom.
（媽，再見。）

單字

again [ə′gen] 再度；又	**close** [kloz] 動 （商店）打烊
busy [′bɪzɪ] 忙的	**early** [′ɝlɪ] 早
sale [sel] 拍賣	**get off** 離開某地

around [ə'raʊnd] （時間）前後；大約	**anyway** ['ɛnɪˌwe] 反正
library ['laɪˌbrɛrɪ] 名 圖書館	**pizza** ['pɪzə] 披薩餅
actually ['æktʃʊəlɪ] 副 實際上；事實上	**order** ['ɔrdɚ] 動 點菜

文法解析

1. 時態

1.a. 過去式

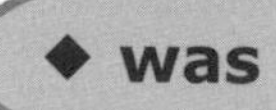

I was up most of the night.
（我整晚幾乎沒睡。）

He was in Hong Kong last week.
（他上星期在香港。）

She wasn't at home last night.
（她昨晚不在家。）

He was late this morning.

（他今天早上遲到。）

1.b. 未來式

◆ going to

It's going to be very busy.

（今天將會很忙。）

She's going to join the club.

（她將會加入社團。）

He's going to work extra hard.

（他將會加倍努力。）

Lisa's going to make supper for us.

（莉沙會為我們做晚飯。）

2. 助動詞

2.a. Did

Did you sleep well?

（你睡得好嗎？）

Did Victoria drive home?

（維多利亞開車回來嗎？）

Did Michael finish his homework?

（邁克有沒有做完他的功課？）

Did he pick you up?

（他有沒有去接你？）

2.b. Do

Do you have to work?

（你必須去上班嗎？）

Do you want to order a pizza?

（你要叫比薩餅嗎？）

Do they like their gift?

（他們喜歡他們的禮物嗎？）

Do you feel like going out?

（你想要出去嗎？）

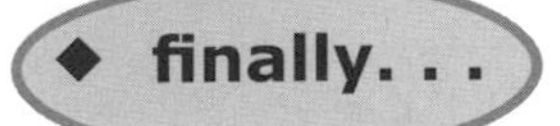

句型練習

◆ finally. . .

I finally finished it.
（我終於做完了。）

He finally got a job.
（他終於找到一份工作。）

They finally called me.
（他們終於打電話給我。）

She finally graduated.
（她終於畢業了。）

◆ I'll see you. . .

I'll see you tonight.
（我們今晚見。）

I'll see you later.
（我們待會兒見。）

I'll see you in the morning.
（我們明天早上見。）

美國口語

◆ Not really

A: Are you ready for your exam?

B: Not really.

I need to study a lot more.

A: 你考試準備好了嗎？

B: 還沒。

我還需要好好讀一讀。

A: Do you like candy?

B: Not really, it is a bit too sweet.

A: 你喜歡糖果嗎？

B: 不是很喜歡，太甜了。

◆ Sounds good.

A: Do you want to go out tonight?

B: Sounds good.

A: 你今晚想出去嗎？

B: 好啊。

A: I'm so hungry for pizza.

B: That sounds good.

We should order one.

A: 我好想吃披薩餅。

B: 好啊。

我們應該叫披薩餅。

◆ You too.

A: Have a good weekend.

B: You too.

A: 祝你這個週末愉快。

B: 你也是。

A: Call me later, John.

You too, George.

B: All right, I'll call you this evening when I get home.

A: 稍後打電話給我，約翰。

喬治，你也一樣。

B: 好的，今晚我回去之後就打電話給你

Lesson 9

中午回家

Lesson 9 中午回家

實用會話 1

MP3 25

Jesse 中午回家吃午飯，現在正準備好要回去上班，他的太太 Lisa 過來跟他談了一下

Jesse Lisa, I'm leaving.
（莉沙，我要走了。）

Lisa Is your lunchtime over already?
（你吃午飯的時間過了嗎？）

Jesse Not yet but I want to get back early.
（還沒有，但是我想早一點回去。）

I have an important meeting and I want some time to prepare for it.
（我有一個很重要的會議，我需要一點時間準備。）

Lisa That's right!
（是啊。）

I forgot all about your meeting today.
（我全忘了你今天的會議。）

Jesse	I wish I could have. （我希望我能忘掉。） I'm really worried. （我真的很擔心。） This is one of our most important clients. （這是我們最重要的客戶之一。）
Lisa	Don't worry, Jesse. I'm sure you'll do fine. （別擔心，傑西，我確定你會做得很好。）
Jesse	Thanks. （謝謝你。）

leave [liv] 離開	**already** [ɔl'rɛdɪ] 副 已經
lunchtime [lʌntʃtaɪm] 午飯時間	**early** ['ɝlɪ] 早
over ['ovɚ] 形 結束	**important** [ɪm'pɔrtənt] 形 重要的

meeting ['mitɪŋ] 會議	**wish** [wɪʃ] 但願；希望
prepare [prɪ'pɛr] 準備	**worried** ['wɝɪd] 憂心；擔心
forgot [fɚ'gɑt] 忘記（forget 的過去式）	**client** ['klaɪənt] 客戶

實用會話 2

Jesse 換個話題，問 Lisa 下午打算作什麼

Jesse	What are you going to do this afternoon? （今天下午你要做什麼？）
Lisa	I'm going grocery shopping. （我要去買點雜貨。） Do you need anything? （你需要什麼東西嗎？）
Jesse	Not really, but I would like some plums. （沒什麼，但是我想要一些李子。）

Lisa	Okay then. （好的。） I'll try to remember to pick some up. （我會盡量記得買一些。）
Jesse	Thanks. （謝謝。） Well, look, I've got to go. （嗯，我該走了。） Tell the kids I love them and I'll be home soon. （跟孩子說，我愛他們，我會很快回來。）
Lisa	I'll do that. （我會的。） Now, get out of here. （快走吧。） Good luck at your meeting and I'll see you tonight. （祝你的會議開得順利，今晚見。）

單字

afternoon [ˌæftɚˈnun] 下午	**remember** [rɪˈmɛmbɚ] 記得
grocery [ˈgrosərɪ] 雜貨；雜貨店	**soon** [sun] 很快地
shopping [ˈʃɑpɪŋ] 購物	**luck** [lʌk] 運氣
need [nid] 需要	**good luck** 祝好運
plum [plʌm] 李子	**tonight** [təˈnaɪt] 今晚

文法解析

1. 時態

1.a. 未來式

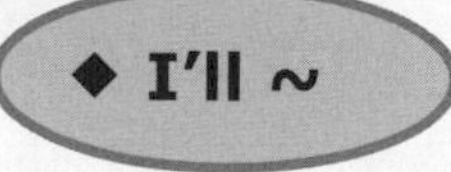

I'll be home soon.

（我會很快回來。）

I'll see you tonight.

（我們今晚見。）

I'll try to remember.

（我會盡力記得。）

I'll do that.

（我會這麼做。）

2. 助動詞

2.a. could

I wish I could forget.

（我希望我能夠忘掉。）

I could go with you.

（我可以跟你一塊去。）

I could help him.

（我可以幫他的忙。）

I could stay here.

（我可以留在這裡。）

3. 命令句

3.a. 命令句（肯定）

Tell the kids I love them.

（跟孩子說，我愛他們。）

Get out of here.

（快走吧。）

Call me after a while.

（待會兒打電話給我。）

3.b. 命令句（否定）

◆ **Don't ~**

Don't worry.

（別擔心。）

Don't forget.

（不要忘記。）

Don't talk.

（不要說話。）

Don't cry.

（別哭。）

句型練習

◆ I'm really ~

I'm really worried.
（我真的很擔心。）

I'm really hungry.
（我真的很餓。）

I'm really tired.
（我真的很疲倦。）

I'm really sick.
（我病得很嚴重。）

◆ Is ~ already

Is your lunchtime over already?
（你的午飯時間過了嗎？）

Is the movie already over?
（電影演完了嗎？）

Is your homework already finished?

（你的功課做完了嗎？）

Is John here already?

（約翰已經到了嗎？）

美國口語

◆ I'll do that.

A: Be sure to finish your homework.

B: I will.

A: And take out the trash too, please.

B: Okay, I'll do that.

A: 一定要把功課做完。

B: 我會的。

A: 還有，要把垃圾拿出去。

B: 好的，我會做。

A: Someone needs to bring the plants in and feed the dog.

B: I'll do that.

A: Great, thank you.

A: 我需要有人把花拿進來，還要餵狗。

B: 我會做。

A: 很好，謝謝你。

◆ Good luck

A: I've got to get this project finished by Friday.

B: Good luck!

A: 星期五之前我得把這個企畫做完。

B: 祝你做得完。

A: Good luck on your exam.

B: Thanks, good luck to you, too.

A: 祝你考試考的好。

B: 謝謝，也祝你考得好。

◆ That's right!

A: Did you forget something today?

B: That's right!

I was supposed to pick you up at the airport.

A: 你今天是不是忘記什麼事？

B: 是的。

我應該到機場接你的。

A: Don't you remember Patrick?

B: That's right!

We met him at a party last year.

A: 你不記得派崔立克？

B: 我想起來了。

去年我們在宴會中遇過他。

Lesson 10

逛街

Lesson 10 逛街

實用會話 1

MP3 27

Helen 帶她的女兒 Victoria 去逛街，她們逛了一整天，非常愉快，現在她們停下來休息吃午飯，順便聊聊天

Victoria	Thanks for taking me **shopping**, mom. （媽，謝謝你帶我逛街。） I'm really having a great time. （我玩得很愉快。）
Helen	It's my pleasure, Victoria. （我很樂意這麼做，維多利亞。） I missed you a lot. （我很想念你。） Besides, sometimes I like for us to just have a day together. （而且，有時我喜歡我們能有一天的時間在一起。） You're a great kid and you're lots of fun. （你是個好孩子，而且跟你在一起很有趣。）

Victoria	Thanks, mom. （謝謝你，媽。） You're fun, too. （你也是很有趣。） Now, what are we going to do next? （現在，我們接下來要做什麼呢？）
Helen	I don't know. （我不知道。）

單字

shopping [ˈʃɑpɪŋ] 購物	**together** [təˈgɛðɚ] 一起
pleasure [ˈplɛʒɚ] 榮幸	**kid** [kɪd] 小孩子
miss [mɪs] 動 想念	**fun** [fʌn] 好玩；樂趣
sometimes [ˈsʌmˈtaɪmz] 有時	**next** [nɛkst] 下一個

實用會話 2

Helen 建議 Victoria 去剪個髮型，Victoria 不想剪頭髮，她想把頭髮留長，接著她們討論還要買什麼東西

Helen

Do you want to get your hair done?
（你要不要去做頭髮？）

I bet May could give you a nice cut.
（我說，梅可以為你剪個漂亮的髮型。）

Victoria

I don't know if I want to get a haircut.
（我不知道我是否要新髮型。）

Then again, I really like what Miss May did with your hair.
（但是，我真的喜歡梅為你做的髮型。）

Still, I think I'm going to grow mine out.
（但是，我想我還是把我的頭髮留長好了。）

But I did think of something I wanted.
（但是，我卻想到我要什麼了。）

Helen

What's that?
（是什麼？）

Victoria

I need a new bathing suit.
（我需要一件新的浴袍。）

I also need a new pair of shoes.
（我也需要一雙新鞋子。）

Helen

No problem.
（沒問題。）

We'll get them after lunch.
（我們吃過午飯就去買。）

I'd like to find you a couple of dresses, too.
（我也想幫你找幾件洋裝。）

hair [hɛr] 頭髮	**again** [ə'gen] 再度；又
bet [bɛt] 動 打賭	**grow** [gro] 留長
haircut ['hɛrˌkʌt] 剪頭髮	**bathing suit** 浴袍

單 字

pair [pɛr] 一雙	**problem** [ˈprɑbləm] 問題
shoes [ʃuz] 鞋子	**dress** [drɛs] 洋裝

MP3 28

實用會話 3

談完了要買的東西，Helen 問起 Victoria 學校的情形

Helen But anyway, tell me, how's school been?
（但是，無論如何，告訴我，你學校的情形怎麼樣？）

Victoria It's crazy!
（簡直忙瘋了。）

This year has been such a mess.
（今年一切亂糟糟的。）

I never seem to get all of my school work done.
（我似乎沒有把所有的學校功課做好。）

Michael and I have been working on this huge project for weeks.
（邁克和我做這個研究作業已經做了好幾個星期了。）

It's almost due and we're not even halfway done yet.
（快要到期了，我們還沒做好一半。）

Helen Are you going to work on it again tonight?
（你今晚還要做嗎？）

Victoria I don't know yet.
（我還不知道。）

It depends on what time Michael gets off work.
（要看邁克什麼時候下班。）

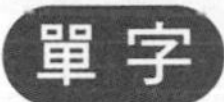

anyway [ˈɛnɪwe] 無論如何	**huge** [hjudʒ] 廣大的
crazy [ˈkrezɪ] 形 瘋狂的	**project** [ˈprɑdʒɛkt] 學校研究作業

單字

mess [mɛs] 亂七八糟；一團糟	**almost** [ˈɔlˌmost] 副 幾乎
due [dju] 到期；期限截止	**yet** [jɛt] 副 尚未
halfway [ˈhæfwe] 到一半	**depend** [dɪˈpɛnd] 動 視～而定

實用會話 4

接著，Helen 話題又轉到她想要去上美術課，畫畫當消遣

Helen	Oh, I need some new paints. （噢，我需要一些水彩。）
Victoria	For what? （做什麼用？） You don't paint. （你又不畫圖。）
Helen	I think I'm going to take an art class for fun. （我想我要去修一門美術課，只是好玩。）

	Your dad will be out of town for two weeks. （你爸爸要出差兩個星期。） If I'm not doing anything, I'll get bored. （如果我不找些事情來做，我會很無聊。）
Victoria	You're always doing something, mom. （媽，你總是會找事情來做。）
Helen	I know. （我知道。） I'm like you, Victoria, I like to stay busy. （我跟你一樣，維多利亞，我喜歡忙碌。）

單字

new [nju] 新的	**art** [ɑrt] 藝術
paint [pent] 名 水彩	**bored** [bord] 無聊的
paint [pent] 動 繪畫	**busy** [ˈbɪzɪ] 忙的

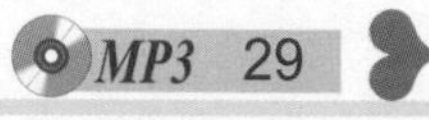

文法解析

1. 時態

1.a. 現在完成進行式

◆ have been+ ~ing

Michael and I have been working on this for weeks.

（邁克和我做這個研究作業已經做了好幾個星期了。）

We have been planning to take a trip.

（我們一直在計畫去旅行。）

It's been raining for hours.

（雨已經下了好幾個小時。）

2. 助動詞

We will get them after lunch.

（我們午飯後去拿。）

Dad will be out of town.

（爸爸要出差去。）

I will get bored.

（我會很無聊。）

I will write you.

（我會寫信給你。）

句型練習

◆ I don't know

I don't know if I want to get a haircut.

（我不知道我是否想剪頭髮。）

I don't know if we're working late.

（我不知道我們是否會工作到很晚）。

I don't know how to do that.

（我不知道怎麼做。）

I don't know the man in the blue shirt.

（我不認識穿藍色襯衫的那個人。）

美國口語

◆ I bet

A: I bet she's a good dancer.

B: I've seen her dance before.

She's pretty good.

A: 我說她一定是個好舞蹈員。

B: 我以前看過她跳舞。

她是跳得很好。

A: I bet I'm going to be late.

B: Not if you hurry.

You still have fifteen minutes.

A: 我說我一定會遲到。

B: 如果你快一點，就不會。

你還有十五分鐘。

◆ My pleasure

A: Thanks for all the help.

B: Oh, it was my pleasure.

A: 謝謝你的幫忙。

B: 能幫你忙是我的榮幸。

A: You've done so much for me.
How can I repay you?

B: Don't worry about it.
It was my pleasure.

A: 你為我做了真多。
我要怎麼報答你？

B: 別擔心。
能幫你忙是我的榮幸。

◆ Crazy

A: Can you believe he said that to me?

B: That's crazy!

He doesn't know what he's talking about.

A: 你會相信他對我這麼說嗎？

B: 真是瘋了。

他不知道他在說什麼。

A: I've been so busy; I haven't even sat down all day.

B: I know what you mean.

It's been crazy here, too.

A: 我一直很忙，我一整天甚至於還沒有坐下來。

B: 我知道你的意思。

我這裡也是一片忙亂。

◆ Such a mess

A: This place is such a mess.

I'll be cleaning all weekend.

B: Don't worry; I'll help you.

A: 這個地方真亂。

我要花整個週末的時間來整理。

B: 別擔心，我會來幫你的忙。

A: How's your project coming along?

B: It's such a mess!

It isn't working out at all.

A: 你的企畫做的怎麼樣？

B: 亂七八糟。

完全沒有做出來。

◆ I don't know yet

A: Are you coming to the party?

B: I don't know yet.

I have to see if I'm free.

A: 你要來參加宴會嗎？

B: 我還不知道。

我要看看我是否有時間。

A: What did the doctor tell him about his chest pains?

B: I don't know yet.

He hasn't called me.

A: 有關他的胸部痛，醫生怎麼說？

B: 我還不知道。

他還沒有打電話給我。

Lesson 11
買東西

Lesson 11 買東西

MP3 30

實用會話 1

Karen 到雜貨店去，想買一些東西，可以讓 Michael 自己煮來吃

Mr. Woods	Karen, how are you? （凱倫，你好嗎？） I haven't seen you in a while. （我有好一陣子沒看到你了。）
Karen	I'm just fine, Mr. Woods. （伍德先生，我很好。） Thank you for asking. （謝謝你的問候。） How have you been? （你這一向可好？）
Mr. Woods	I've just been keeping busy. （我就是這麼忙。） Mary and I work all the time. （瑪麗和我總是忙著工作。）

Karen	I've been working a lot myself. （我自己也是很忙。） In fact, I've been home late every day this week. （事實上，我這個星期每天都很晚回家。）
Mr. Woods	It sounds like that new boss is keeping you busy. （看起來，你的新老闆讓你很忙。）
Karen	Yes, but I don't mind. （是的，但是我不介意。） I just wish I had more time to spend with Michael. （我只是希望，我能有多一點的時間陪邁克。） He's growing up fast. （他長的好快。）
Mr. Woods	Kids always do. （小孩子都是這樣。） Can I help you find anything special today? （你需要我幫你找什麼東西嗎？）

Karen

Actually I just want to pick up a few things.
（事實上，我只是想買幾樣東西。）

I'm trying to find stuff that's easy for Michael to cook.
（我想找簡單的，邁克可以煮的東西。）

That way I know he eats even if I have to work late.
（那樣，即使我上班到很晚，我知道他有吃東西。）

單字

while [hwaɪl] 一段時間	**myself** [maɪ'sɛlf] 我自己
busy ['bɪzɪ] 忙的	**late** [let] 形 很晚
work [wɝk] 動 工作	**boss** [bɔs] 名 主管；老闆

mind [maɪnd] 動 介意	**special** [ˈspɛʃəl] 形 特別
spend [spɛnd] 動 花（時間）	**actually** [ˈæktʃʊəlɪ] 副 實際上；事實上
fast [fæst] 快	**stuff** [stʌf] 名 物品；東西
kid [kɪd] 小孩子	**easy** [ˈizɪ] 形 容易的；簡單的
always [ˈɔlwez] 總是	**cook** [kʊk] 動 烹調；煮

實用會話 2

雜貨店老闆伍德先生推薦一些簡單容易煮的食品給 Karen

Mr. Woods We have those frozen dinners on sale this week.
（我們有這些冷凍晚餐這個星期正在打折拍賣。）

They're only 2 for $5.00.
（兩個只要五塊錢美金。）

Karen	Wow, that's a really good price. （哇，價錢真的很好。） I think I'll pick up a few of them. （我想我要買幾個。） That way he can just put them in the microwave when he's ready to eat. （那樣，他想吃的時候就可以放到微波爐去。。）
Mr. Woods	That sounds good. （很好。） They're on aisle seven. （在第七排。）
Karen	Thanks a lot for your help. （多謝你的幫忙。）
Mr. Woods	Anytime, Karen. （別客氣。）

frozen ['frozn̩] 冷凍的	**dinner** ['dɪnɚ] 晚餐；正餐

on sale 拍賣	microwave [ˈmaɪkrəˌwev] 微波爐
really [ˈriəlɪ] 真的	ready [ˈrɛdɪ] 準備好
price [praɪs] 價格	aisle [aɪl] （貨架的）行列

文法解析

1. 時態

1.a. 現在完成式（否定句）

◆ Have (not) ~

I haven't seen you in a while.
（我有一段時間沒有看到你。）

I haven't read that book.
（我還沒看那本書。）

I haven't eaten yet.
（我還沒吃飯。）

I haven't been here in years.
（我好幾年沒來這裡了。）

句型練習

◆ pick up

I just want to pick up a few things.

（我只是想買幾樣東西。）

I need to pick up my dry cleaning.

（我需要去拿乾洗的衣物。）

Ask him to pick up the cake and the balloons.

（叫他去拿蛋糕和氣球。）

◆ anything special

Can I help you find anything special?

（你要買什麼特別的東西，需要我幫你找嗎？）

Are you looking for anything special today?

（你今天要買什麼特別的東西嗎？）

◆ I wish

I wish I had more time to spend with Michael.

（我希望我能有更多的時間陪邁克。）

I wish my mom would let me have a dog.

（我希望我媽媽能讓我養狗。）

美國口語

◆ Anytime

A: When can I stop by to pick up those papers?

B: Anytime.

I'll be home all afternoon.

A: 我什麼時候可以過來拿那些報告？

B: 隨時都行。

我整個下午都在。

A: Thanks for taking me to the zoo.

B: Anytime.

It was lots of fun.

A: 謝謝你帶我去動物園。

B: 別客氣。

我們玩得很愉快。

◆ Sounds like a plan

A: I want to go to the movies tonight.

B: Sounds like a plan.

When should I pick you up?

A: 我今晚要去看電影。

B: 聽起來是個好計畫。

我幾點來接你？

A: I need you to help me decorate for the surprise party.

B: Sounds like a plan.
I'll be here as soon as I get out of work.

A: 我需要你幫我裝飾驚奇宴會的會場。
B: 聽起來是個好計畫。
我一下班就會盡快趕過來。

Memo

Lesson 12

看電影

Lesson 12

看電影

實用會話 1

MP3 32

Brandon 想要看電影錄影帶，他問媽媽可不可以看

Brandon	Mom, can I watch a movie? （媽，我可以看電影嗎？）
Lisa	I don't know, Brandon. （我不知道，布藍登。） Is your homework done? （你的功課做完了嗎？）
Brandon	Almost. （快做完了。） I've only got one problem left. （只剩下一個問題。）
Lisa	Well, I guess it would be okay. （那，我想你應該可以看。）
Brandon	Thanks. （謝謝。）

	Will you help me put it on? （你可以幫我放錄影帶放進去嗎？）
Lisa	Okay, what movie did you want to watch? （好的，你想看那一部電影？）
Brandon	I was thinking about watching Robin Hood. （我想看『羅賓漢』。）

單字

watch [watʃ] 觀看	**problem** [ˈprabləm] 問題
movie [ˈmuvɪ] 電影	**left** [lɛft] 剩下的
homework [ˈhomˈwɝk] 家庭作業	**guess** [gɛs] 猜想
almost [ˈɔlˌmost] 副 幾乎	**help** [hɛlp] 幫助

實用會話 2

Brandon 的小妹妹 Jennifer 一聽到他哥哥要看羅賓漢，她也要看

Jennifer I love Robin Hood!
（我喜歡『羅賓漢』。）

Can I watch it too, mom?
（媽，我也可以看嗎？）

Lisa I think that would be great.
（我想應該可以。）

Ask your brother what he thinks.
（問你哥哥看他怎麼說。）

Jennifer Brandon, can I watch Robin Hood with you?
（布藍登，我可以跟你一起看『羅賓漢』嗎？）

Brandon Sure, but try not to talk.
（可以，但是盡量不要說話。）

You have to be quiet during the movie.
（看電影時要很安靜。）

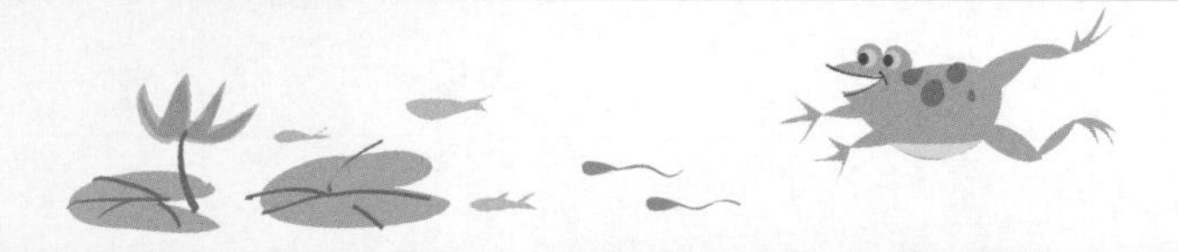

Jennifer	I won't talk at all, I promise. （我保證，我不會說話。）
Lisa	Okay, you two. （好了，你們兩個。） Here you go. （電影開始了。）
Brandon	Thanks, Mom. （謝謝。）
Lisa	No problem. （別客氣。） Enjoy your movie. （享受你們的電影吧。）

單字

try [traɪ] 嘗試	**during** [ˈdjʊrɪŋ] 介 在～的期間
talk [tɔk] 說話	**promise** [ˈprɑmɪs] 保證；答應
quiet [ˈkwaɪət] 安靜的	**enjoy** [ɪnˈdʒɔɪ] 享受

MP3 33 

文法解析

1. 時態

1.a. 過去進行式

◆ was +ing

I was thinking about watching Robin Hood.
（我想要看『羅賓漢』。）

I was planning on going shopping today.
（我計畫今天去購物。）

She was hoping you would call.
（她希望你會打電話給她。）

2. 助動詞

2.a. Will

Will you help me put it on?
（你可以幫我穿上這件嗎？）

Will you tell me a bedtime story?
（你可以跟我說個睡前故事嗎？）

Will you take me to the park?

（你可以帶我去公園嗎？）

Will you draw a picture for me?

（你可以幫我畫個圖嗎？）

2.b. Can

Can I watch a movie?

（我可以看電影嗎？）

Can I go to the mall?

（我可以去購物中心嗎？）

Can I take the dog for a walk?

（我可以帶狗去散步嗎？）

Can I go over to Mary's?

（我可以去瑪麗家嗎？）

句型練習

◆ I guess

I guess it would be okay.

（我想應該沒有問題。）

I guess I'd better go or I'll be late.

（我想我該走了，否則我會遲到。）

I guess I'll see you sometime soon.

（我想我很快會再見到你。）

美國口語

◆ Almost.

A: Are you finished yet?

B: Almost.

I just need a few more minutes.

A: 你做完了嗎？

B: 快做完了。

我只要再幾分鐘。

A: Has Michael finished reading that book?

B: Almost.

He's on the last chapter.

A: 邁克那本書看玩了嗎？

B: 快玩了。

他在看最後一章。

◆ Here you go.

A: Can I have some cookies?

B: Here you go.

Share them with your friend.

A: 我可以吃一些餅乾嗎？

B: 在這裡。

跟你的朋友一起吃。

A: Can you hand me that?

B: Here you go.

A: Thanks.

A: 你可以把那個遞給我嗎？

B 在這裡。

A: 謝謝你。

◆ No Problem.

A: Thanks for helping me move.

B: No problem.

That's what friends are for.

A: 謝謝你幫我搬家。

B: 沒問題。

朋友就是該這麼做。

A: Can I get you anything?

B: I don't want you to trouble yourself.

A: It's no problem.

Really, I don't mind.

A: 你要我拿什麼東西給你嗎？

B: 我不要你太麻煩。

A: 沒關係的。

真的，我不怕麻煩。

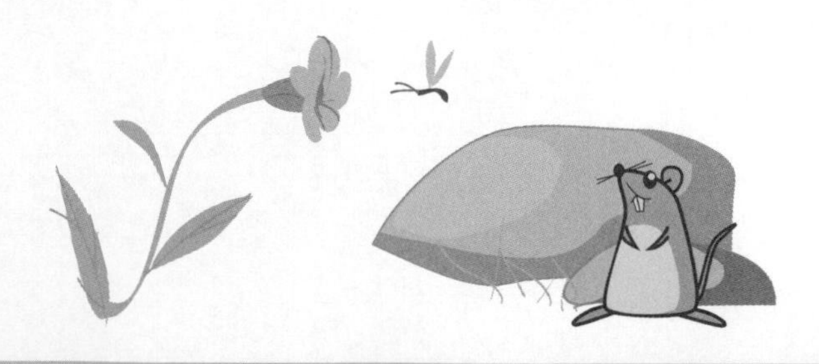

Lesson 13

下班回家

Lesson 13 下班回家

MP3 34

實用會話 1

Jesse 很晚才下班回來，他的太太 Lisa 問他上班的情形怎麼樣

Lisa	Hey, how was your day? （嗨，今天怎麼樣？）
Jesse	Long. Very long. （今天真是忙死了。） How about yours? （你今天怎麼樣？）
Lisa	It was okay. （還好。） I did some shopping and I talked to Karen. （我去買了些東西，還跟凱倫講了話。） She says to tell you hi. （她要我跟你問好。）

We are going to have lunch together on Saturday.
（我們星期六要一起去吃午飯。）

Jesse That's great.
（那很好。）

I'm glad she called.
（我很高興她打電話來。）

Next time you talk to her, tell her I said hi back.
（下一次，你跟她談話時，替我跟她問好。）

Lisa I'll do that.
（我會的。）

But tell me about your day.
（告訴我，你今天怎麼樣？）

Nothing bad happened at the meeting, did it?
（會議上沒有什麼不好的消息吧？）

Jesse No, nothing bad.
（沒有，沒有什麼不好的。）

It's just that our client won't commit.
（只是我們的客戶不願簽約。）

	He keeps changing his demands. （他一直更改他的要求。） We can't seem to satisfy him. （我們好像沒辦法滿足他。）
Lisa	Well, try not to worry about it too much. （嗯，別太擔心。） Some people are just like that. （有些人就是那樣。） I'm sure things will get better soon. （我確信，事情很快會好轉。）
Jesse	I hope you're right. （我希望你說的對。） I'd like to finish up this account by the end of the week. （我想要這個週末之前把這個帳戶搞定。）

單字

shopping [ˈʃɑpɪŋ] 購物	**together** [təˈgɛðɚ] 一起

Saturday [ˈsætɚde] 星期六	**satisfy** [ˈsætɪsfaɪ] 動 滿意
call [kɔl] 打電話	**seem** [sim] 似乎
next time 下一次	**try** [traɪ] 嘗試
happen [ˈhæpən] 發生	**worry** [ˈwɝɪ] 動 憂慮；擔心
meeting [ˈmitɪŋ] 會議	**soon** [sun] 很快地
bad [bæd] 不好	**right** [raɪt] 對的
client [ˈklaɪənt] 客戶	**finish** [ˈfɪnɪʃ] 完成
commit [kəˈmɪt] 動 承諾	**account** [əˈkaʊnt] 名 帳戶
change [tʃendʒ] 改變；變更	**end** [ɛnd] 結束
demand [dɪˈmænd] 名 要求	**week** [wik] 星期

實用會話 2

談完工作，Jesse 就問起孩子們怎麼樣

Jesse	So, are the kids in bed? （那，孩子上床了嗎？）
Lisa	Yes, they've already gone to bed. （是，他們已經上床了。） But I doubt they're asleep. （但是，我懷疑他們已經睡了。）
Jesse	Good, I'm going to go peek in on them. （好，我要去瞧瞧。） Maybe I'll tell them a story if they're still awake. （如果他們還醒著，我或許會講個睡前故事給他們聽。）
Lisa	I think they'd like that a lot. （我想他們會很喜歡。）
Jesse	Okay, I'll be back downstairs in a minute. （好的，我一下就下樓來。）

Lisa

Take your time.
（不用急。）

While you visit with them, I'll heat your dinner up.
（你去看他們的時間我會把你的晚餐熱一下。）

單字

kid [kɪd] 小孩子	**still** [stɪl] 副 仍然
go to bed 上床睡覺	**awake** [ɔ'wek] 醒著
already [ɔl'rɛdɪ] 副 已經	**downstairs** ['daʊn'stɛrz] 樓下的
doubt [daʊt] 動 懷疑	**while** [hwaɪl] 當…的時候
asleep [ə'slip] 形 睡著的	**heat** [hit] 動 加熱
peek [pik] 偷瞧	**dinner** ['dɪnɚ] 晚餐

MP3 35

文法解析

1. 時態

1.a. 未來式

◆ **are going to + 原形動詞**

We are going to have lunch together.
（我們要一起去吃午飯。）

They are going to visit their grandparents.
（他們要去拜訪他們的祖父母。）

He is going to see the dentist on Tuesday.
（他星期二要去看牙醫。）

We are going to have a party this Friday.
（我們這個星期五有個宴會。）

2. 助動詞

2.a. can 的否定句

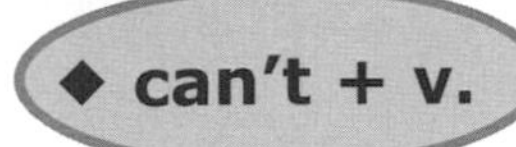

We can't seem to satisfy him.
（我們好像沒辦法使他滿足。）

I can't blow up another balloon.
（我沒辦法再吹另一個氣球。）

He can't come this evening.
（他今晚不能來。）

He can't swim.
（他不會游泳。）

句型練習

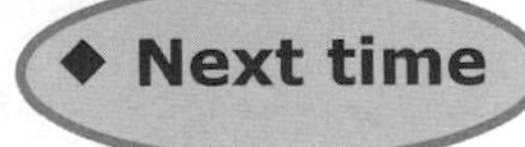

Next time you talk to her, tell her I said hi.
（下一次你跟她說話時，跟她說我跟她問好。）

Next time you call, I'll give you my answer.
（下一次，你打電話來時，我會給你答案。）

◆ Did it

Nothing bad happened at the meeting, did it?
（會議上沒有什麼不好的事情發生吧？）

That didn't hurt, did it?
（不會痛吧？）

It didn't break, did it?
（沒有打破吧？）

◆ Maybe

Maybe I'll tell them a story.
（或許我會說個故事給他們聽。）

Maybe I'll call you later.
（或許我稍後會打電話給你。）

Maybe she can come with us.

（或許他可以跟我們一起來。）

Maybe we should go now.

（或許我們現在該走了。）

美國口語

◆ Some people are just like that.

A: My teacher is always mad.

B: Don't worry about it.

Some people are just like that.

A: 我們老師一天到晚在生氣。

B: 別擔心。

有些人就是那樣。

A: Why does he always make fun of everything?

B: Some people are just like that.

A: 他為什麼總是嘲笑天下事？

B: 有些人就是那樣。

◆ Peek in on. . .

A: What are the kids doing?

B: I don't know.

Peek in on them and see.

A: 孩子們在做什麼？

B: 我不知道。

你去瞧瞧。

A: How do you know what we're having for dinner?

B: I just peeked in on mom and saw her making it.

A: 你怎麼知道我們晚飯要吃什麼？

B: 我去偷瞧媽在做什麼。

Lesson 14
學校成績

Lesson 14 學校成績

實用會話 1

MP3 36

Karen 和她兒子 Michael 在討論 Michael 的成績單

Karen	How was school today, Michael? （邁克，學校裡怎麼樣？）
Michael	It was all right. （還好。） I got my report card. （我拿到成績單了。）
Karen	Really? （真的？） How'd you do? （成績怎麼樣？）
Michael	I did okay. （還好。） I got two A's and three B's. （我拿到兩科 A，三科 B。）

單字

report card	really ['riəlɪ]
成績單	真的

實用會話 2

Karen 得知 Michael 的成績之後，非常高興，雖然 Michael 沒有拿到全 A 的成績，但是因為 Michael 必須一邊打工，一邊讀書，所以 Karen 認為 Michael 得到的成績很好

Karen

Wow, Michael, that's very good.
（哇，邁克，那很好。）

I'm really proud of you.
（我真以你為傲。）

You're such a smart boy.
（你真是個聰明的孩子。）

Michael

Thanks, mom.
（謝謝你，媽媽。）

But really, I'm not that smart.
（但是，我真的沒那麼聰明。）

Karen No, I mean it.
（不，我是說真的。）

You've always been smart.
（你一向都很聰明。）

單字

proud [praʊd] 感到驕傲	**mean** [min] 意思是
smart [smɑrt] 聰明的	**always** ['ɔlwez] 總是

MP3 37

實用會話 3

Karen 建議帶 Michael 出去吃晚餐，慶祝 Michael 的好成績，但是 Michael 已經跟 Victoria 約好要一起做學校的研究作業

Karen We should celebrate.
（我們應該慶祝一下。）

Why don't we go out to dinner?
（我們何不出去吃晚飯？）

Michael

I'd love to, mom, but I can't tonight.
（我是很想去，但是今天晚上不行。）

I've got to meet Victoria at the library.
（我必須在圖書館跟維多利亞見面。）

Our paper is due in three days and it's really tough.
（我們的報告三天內要交，這篇報告很難。）

We've been working on it; but it's not getting anywhere.
（我們一直在做這個報告，但是卻沒有進展。）

Karen

That's okay. I understand.
（沒關係，我瞭解。）

Maybe we can do it another time.
（或許，我們可以改天再一起出去吃飯。）

Hey, I have an idea.
（對了，我有個主意。）

Why don't you invite Victoria to dinner with us?
（你何不邀請維多利亞跟我們去吃晚餐？）

You can discuss your paper there.
（你可以在吃飯時跟她討論報告。）

Michael	I don't know, mom. （我不知道，媽。） Are you sure? （你認為這樣好嗎？）
Karen	Of course I'm sure. （我當然認為很好。） Now call your friend and invite her to dinner. （去打電話給你的朋友，邀她吃晚飯。）

單字

celebrate [ˈsɛləˌbret] 慶祝	**due** [dju] 到期；期限截止
tonight [təˈnaɪt] 今晚	**tough** [tʌf] （口語）艱難
library [ˈlaɪˌbrɛrɪ] 名 圖書館	**anywhere** [ˈɛnɪhwɛr] 多少有點進展
meet [mit] 見面	**understand** [ˌʌndɚˈstænd] 瞭解；明白

invite [ɪn'vaɪt] 邀請	sure [ʃʊr] 形 的確的；確定；毫無疑問的
discuss [dɪ'skʌs] 動 討論；商量	of course 當然

文法解析

1. 時態

1.a. 過去式

◆ How did

How'd you do?

（你做得怎麼樣？）

How'd you like it?

（那個你喜歡嗎？）

How'd he fall down?

（他怎麼跌倒的？）

How'd she know about that?

（她怎麼知道的？）

1.b. 現在式

Our paper is due in three days.

（我們的報告三天內到期。）

She is ready to go.

（她準備好可以走了。）

That is sad to hear.

（聽到這件事，真遺憾。）

He is sorry for saying that.

（他對於他那麼說，很抱歉。）

助動詞

2.a. Should

We should celebrate.

（我們應該慶祝。）

You should share your toys.

（你們的玩具應該一起玩。）

We should eat more vegetables.

（我們應該多吃一些蔬菜。）

You should give him a call.

（你應該打電話給他。）

句型練習

◆ Why don't . . .?

Why don't we go out to dinner?

（我們何不出去吃晚飯？）

Why don't you invite Victoria?

（你何不邀請維多利亞？）

Why don't you tell me about it?

（你何不把那件事跟我說？）

Why don't they ever visit?

（他們為何從不來拜訪一下？）

◆ always

You've always been smart.

（你一直都是這麼聰明。）

She's always been sweet.

（她一直都很乖。）

They've always wanted a puppy.

（他們一直都想要一隻寵物。）

I've always liked that song.

（我一直都很喜歡那首歌。）

◆ Are you sure?

A: Helen is back in town.

B: Are you sure?

A: Yes, I saw her at the beauty shop.

A: 海倫回來了。

B: 你確定嗎？

A: 是的，我在美容院看到她。

A: No thanks, I don't want any.

B: Are you sure?

They're really good.

A: 不用了，謝謝，我不需要。

B: 你確定嗎？

這些很好的。

◆ I've got to.

A: Please don't work this weekend.

B: I've got to.

I need to finish this project by next week.

A: 這個週末請不要工作。

B: 我不工作不行。

下個星期之前我必須完成這個企畫。

A: Why don't you come with us?

B: I've got to stay here and wait for my mom.

A: 你何不跟我們一起來？

B 我必須留在這裡等我媽媽。

◆ I understand

A: I'm sorry I couldn't help you.

B: It's okay, I understand.

A: 很抱歉，我幫不上你的忙。

B: 沒關係，我瞭解。

A: I wish I could go but I already have plans.

B: I understand.

Maybe you can come next time.

A: 我希望我能去，但是，我另外有事。

B: 我瞭解。

或許你下次能來。

Lesson 15

到冰淇淋店

Lesson 15 到冰淇淋店

MP3 39

實用會話 1

Victoria 和 Michael 在一起做功課，他們決定該是回家的時候了，他們打算先到冰淇淋店去吃冰，然後再回家

Michael	I think our report is going to be great. （我想我們的報告應該會很好。）
Victoria	I know. （我知道。） This is such an inteesting topic. （這是個很有趣的主題。） But I just can't study any more. （但是，我想讀的差不多了。） I'm starving. （我快餓死了。）
Michael	Me too. （我也是。） Why don't we go get some ice cream? （我們何不去吃冰淇淋？）

Victoria That sound's like a great idea.
（聽起來是個好主意。）

Michael Good then.
（那很好。）

Come on.
（走吧。）

實用會話 2

他們來到冰淇淋店，邁克跟冰店主人 Mr. Jones 打招呼

Michael Hey Mr. Jones.
（嗨，瓊斯先生。）

Mr. Jones Hey Michael.
（嗨，邁克。）

Hello Victoria.
（哈囉，維多利亞）

You look lovely today.
（你今天很漂亮。）

Victoria	Thanks, Mr. Jones. （謝謝你，瓊斯先生。）
Mr. Jones	What are you kids up to today? （你們兩個今天想吃什麼？）
Victoria	We've been at the library working on a report. （我們一直在圖書館做研究報告。）
Mr. Jones	Well, then I know you must need some ice cream. （那，我知道你們一定需要一些冰淇淋。）

實用會話 3

冰店主人 Mr. Jones 問 Michael 和 Victoria 要吃什麼冰淇淋

Mr. Jones	Michael, do you want the usual? （邁克，你要你平常吃的那種嗎？）
Michael	That sounds good. （很好。）

Mr. Jones	Okay, it's coming. （好的，就來了。） And you, Victoria? （你呢，維多利亞？） Will you have the same? （你也要相同的嗎？）
Victoria	Actually, I think I'm going to try something new. （事實上，我想我要試試新的。） I think I want a Lemon-flavored ice cream. （我要檸檬味道的冰淇淋。）
Mr. Jones	That's an excellent choice. （選的好。） It's delicious. （那種很好吃。） Here you go. （在這裡。）
Victoria	Oh, you're right. （噢，你說的對。）

	This is good. （這個很好吃。） Michael, you have to try this. （邁克，你一定要嚐嚐這個。）
Michael	Yummy! （很好吃。） Well, Mr. Jones, thanks for the ice cream. （嗯，瓊斯先生，謝謝你的冰淇淋。） I've got to get home because I'm having dinner with my mom. （我要回家了，因為我要跟我媽媽去吃晚飯。）
Victoria	Yeah, and I've got a French exam to study for. （是啊，而我還有法文的考試需要念。）
Mr. Jones	Well, thanks for coming by. （嗯，謝謝你們來。） It was good seeing you again. （再看到你們真好。） You two have fun and come back any time. （祝你們兩個玩的愉快，隨時再來。）

MP3 41

文法解析

1. 時態

1.a. 現在式

This is such an interesting topic.
（這是一個很有趣的主題。）

It is nice to talk to you.
（跟你談話真好。）

Pizza is delicious.
（披薩餅真好吃。）

Orange is my favorite fruit.
（橘子是我最喜歡的水果。）

句型練習

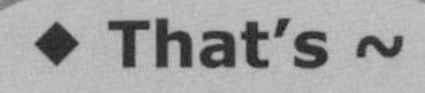

That's an excellent choice.

（那是個很好的選擇。）

That's my favorite.

（那是我最喜歡的。）

That's the one I want.

（那就是我要的。）

◆ Any time.

Come back any time.

（有空隨時回來。）

Call me any time.

（有空打電話來。）

Stop by any time.

（有空過來坐坐。）

Feel free to visit any time you'd like.

（有空隨時歡迎來玩。）

美國口語

◆ Good then.

A: You can come with me.

B: Good then, I will.

A: 你可以跟我一起來。

B: 好的，我就來。

A: Don't forget that we're supposed to have lunch together.

B: Good then, I'll see you Friday.

A: 別忘記，我們說好要一起去吃午飯。

B: 好的，我們星期五見。

◆ Come on.

A: I'd really like to go swimming.

B: Well then, come on.
We'll go to the pool.

A: 我真想去游泳。

B: 那，就走吧。
我們到游泳池去。

A: I just saw Michael walk past here.

B: Come on then, let's see where he's going.

A: 我剛看到邁克從這兒經過。

B: 來吧，我們看看他要去哪裡。

◆ You're right

A: Mr. Lee is always in a good mood.

B: You're right.

That man always seems happy.

A: 李先生總是心情很好。

B: 你說的對。

那個人總是看起來很快樂。

◆ You'll have to try this.

A: I'm hungry for something sweet.

B: Then you'll have to try this.

It's the sweetest candy I've ever had.

A: 我肚子好餓，想吃甜的東西。
B: 那你應該嚐嚐這個。
這是我吃過最甜的糖果。

A: You'll have to try this game.
It's so cool.
B: Then move over and let me have a turn.

A: 你應該試試這個遊戲。
很棒的。
B: 那麼，坐過去一點，讓我玩玩看。

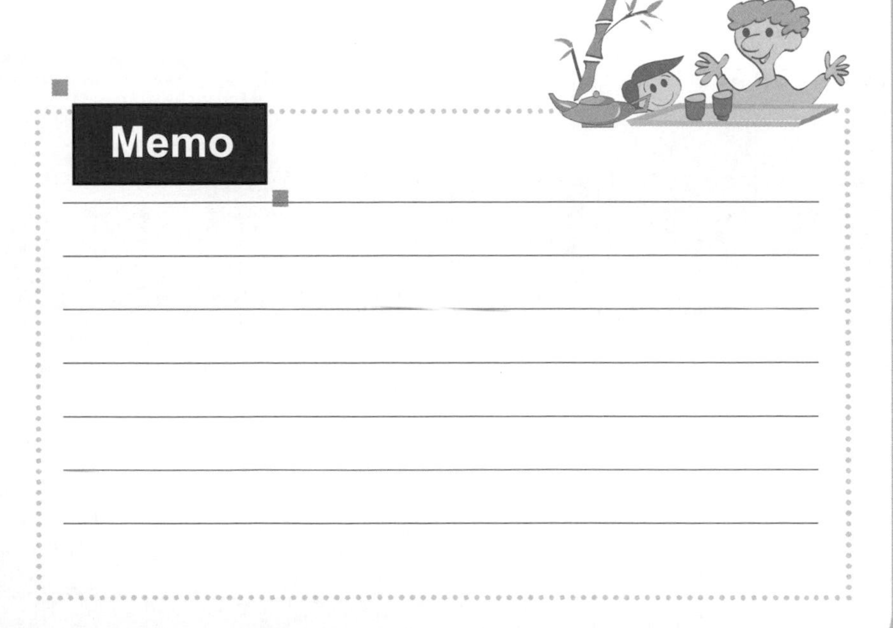

附錄
美國人常用
單字片語
總整理

trip	[trɪp]	旅程；旅遊
wonderful	[ˈwʌndɚfəl]	好棒的；絕妙的；好極了
island	[ˈaɪlənd] n.	島
beautiful	[ˈbjutəfəl] a.	美麗的
wish	[wɪʃ]	希望
weather	[ˈwɛðɚ]	天氣
vacation	[vəˈkeʃən] n.	休假；假期
back	[bæk]	回來
land	[lænd] v.	著陸
pick someone up		接
taxi	[ˈtæksɪ]	計程車
finish	[ˈfɪnɪʃ]	完成
weekend	[ˈwikˈɛnd] n.	週末
zoo	[zu]	動物園
sound	[saʊnd] v.	聽起來
idea	[aɪˈdɪə]	主意；概念
spend	[spɛnd] v.	花（時間）
wait	[wet]	等
anyhow	[ˈɛnɪhau]	不管怎麼說；無論如何
overtime	[ˈovɚˌtaɪm]	加班
seem	[sim]	似乎
earlier	[ˈɝlɪɚ] a.	稍早；較早的；（early 的比較級）
really	[ˈriəlɪ]	真的
library	[ˈlaɪˌbrɛrɪ] n.	圖書館

hard	[hɑrd]	努力的
glad	[glæd]	高興
report	[rɪ'port]	報告
careful	['kɛrfəl]	小心；仔細的
in fact		事實上
miss	[mɪs] v.	想念
think	[θɪŋk]	想
yourself	[jʊr'sɛlf]	你自己
pretty	['prɪtɪ] adv.	非常；相當
great	[gret]	很好
kid	[kɪd]	小孩子
wonderful	['wʌndɚfəl]	好棒的；絕妙的；好極了
still	[stɪl] adv.	仍然
work	[wɝk]	工作
music	['mjuzɪk]	音樂
store	[stor] n.	商店
grade	[gred]	成績
lucky	['lʌkɪ] a.	幸運的
feel	[fil]	感覺
bad	[bæd]	不好
sometimes	['sʌm'taɪmz]	有時
myself	[maɪ'sɛlf]	我自己
worry	['wɝɪ] v.	憂慮
both	[boθ]	兩個…（都）

always	[ˈɔlwez]	總是
easy	[ˈizɪ] a.	容易的
boss	[bɔs] n.	主管；老闆
guy	[gaɪ]	（口語）男士
remember	[rɪˈmɛmbɚ]	記得
jerk	[dʒɝk]	惹人討厭的人
completely	[kəmˈplitlɪ]	完全地
agree	[əˈgri] v.	同意
weekend	[ˈwikˈɛnd]	週末
plan	[plæn]	計畫
fun	[fʌn]	好玩；樂趣
sure	[ʃʊr]	確定
report	[rɪˈport]	報告
recommend	[ˌrɛkəˈmɛnd]	推薦；介紹
useful	[ˈjusfəl]	有用的；有助益的
helpful	[ˈhɛlpfəl] a.	有幫助的
after all		究竟
grade	[gred]	成績
horror	[ˈhɔrɚ]	恐怖
story	[ˈstorɪ]	故事
mystery	[ˈmɪstərɪ] n.	神秘；懸疑
fiction	[ˈfɪkʃən] n.	小說
section	[ˈsɛkʃən]	（零售店的）部門；區域
mummies	[ˈmʌmɪz]	木乃伊（mummy 的複數）

believe	[bɪ'liv] v.	相信
picture	['pɪktʃɚ]	圖畫；相片
sound	[saʊnd] v.	聽起來
interesting	['ɪntrɪstɪŋ]	有趣的
show	[ʃo]	展示；帶領
find	[faɪnd]	找到
trip	[trɪp]	旅程；旅遊
always	['ɔlwez]	總是
scuba diving		潛水
believe	[bɪ'liv] v.	相信
beautiful	['bjutəfəl] a.	美麗的；漂亮的
whole	[hol]	全部的；整體的
wonderful	['wʌndɚfəl]	好棒的；絕妙的；好極了
lucky	['lʌkɪ] a.	幸運的
before	[bɪ'for]	之前
first	[fɝst]	第一次
definitely	['dɛfənətlɪ]	確定地；肯定地
sometime	['sʌmtaɪm]	哪一天；將來某個時候
remind	[rɪ'maɪnd]	提醒
brought	[brɔt] v.	帶來；（bring的過去式，過去分詞）
sweet	[swit]	甜的；可愛的
unusual	[ʌn'juʒʊəl]	不尋常的
ring	[rɪŋ]	戒指
ever	['ɛvɚ] adv.	曾經

completely	[kəm′plitlɪ]	完全地
shell	[ʃɛl]	貝殼
worry	[′wɝɪ] v.	憂慮；擔心
hair	[hɛr]	頭髮
mess	[mɛs]	亂七八糟；一團糟
sand	[sænd] n.	沙
fix	[fɪks]	整理
trim	[trɪm] v.	修剪
party	[′pɑrtɪ]	宴會；派對
idea	[aɪ′dɪə]	主意
actually	[′æktʃʊəlɪ] adv.	實際上；事實上
cavern	[′kævɚn]	洞穴
even	[′ivən]	甚至
zoo	[zu]	動物園
especially	[ə′spɛʃəlɪ]	特別是
break	[brek] n.	短暫的休息
stock	[stɑk]	股票
crazy	[′krezɪ] a.	瘋狂的
market	[′mɑrkɪt]	市場
still	[stɪl] adv.	仍然
invest	[ɪn′vɛst]	投資
save	[sev]	節省
true	[tru]	真的
start	[stɑrt]	開始

hurt	[hɝt]	傷害
allow	[ə'laʊ] v.	允許
investment	[ɪn'vɛstmənt]	投資
truth	[truθ]	實話
hard	[hɑrd]	困難的
broker	['brokɚ]	股票經紀人
meet	[mit]	見面
advice	[əd'vaɪs]	建議
appreciate	[ə'priʃɪˌet] v.	感激
anything	['ɛnɪθɪŋ] adv.	實際上；事實上
actually	['æktʃʊəlɪ] adv.	實際上；事實上
plum	[plʌm]	李子
on sale		拍賣
pound	[paʊnd]	磅
weigh	[we] v.	秤重量
little	['lɪtl̩] a.	小的
start	[stɑrt]	開始
kindergarten	['kɪndɚgɑrtn̩]	幼稚園
why	[hwaɪ]	為什麼
husband	['hʌzbənd]	丈夫
hard	[hɑrd]	努力的
hear	[hɪr]	聽到
favorite	['fevərɪt]	最喜歡的
pie	[paɪ]	（水果）派

recipe	[ˈrɛsəpɪ]	食譜
appreciate	[əˈpriʃɪˌet] v.	感激
come across		偶然遇見
total	[ˈtotḷ]	總共
nice	[naɪs]	很好
ourselves	[aʊrˈsɛlvz]	我們自己
play	[ple] v.	打球；遊玩
maybe	[ˈmebi]	也許
next	[nɛkst]	下一個
turn	[tɝn]	輪流
time	[taɪm]	時間；次
hurt	[hɝt]	傷害
leave	[liv]	留著
alone	[əˈlon] a.	孤單的；單獨的；獨自
leave someone alone		某人 alone 不要去惹某人
minute	[ˈmɪnɪt] n.	（時間單位）分
guess	[gɛs]	猜想
play	[ple]	打球；玩
then	[ðɛn]	然後
inside	[ˈɪnˈsaɪd]	在……的裡面；內部；在屋裡的
let	[lɛt]	讓
friend	[frɛnd]	朋友
without	[wɪðˈaʊt]	沒有

read	[rid]	讀
story	['storɪ]	故事
doll	[dɑl]	娃娃
pick	[pɪk]	挑選
whatever	[hwɑt'ɛvɚ]	任何…的事物
fine	[faɪn]	好吧
sleep	[slip] v.	睡覺
well	[wɛl] adv.	好；適當地
report	[rɪ'port]	報告
finally	['faɪnl̩ɪ]	最終；終於
finish	['fɪnɪʃ]	完成
hard	[hɑrd]	困難的
hang in there		堅持下去
proud	[praʊd]	感到驕傲
again	[ə'gen]	再度；又
busy	['bɪzɪ]	忙的
sale	[sel]	拍賣
close	[kloz] v.	（商店）打烊
early	['ɝlɪ]	早
get off		離開某地
around	[ə'raʊnd]	（時間）前後；大約
library	['laɪˌbrɛrɪ] n.	圖書館
actually	['æktʃʊəlɪ] adv.	實際上；事實上
anyway	['ɛnɪˌwe]	反正

pizza	[ˈpɪzə]	披薩餅
order	[ˈɔrdɚ] v.	點菜
leave	[liv]	離開
lunchtime	[lʌntʃtaɪm]	午飯時間
over	[ˈovɚ] a.	結束
already	[ɔlˈrɛdɪ] adv.	已經
early	[ˈɝlɪ]	早
important	[ɪmˈpɔrtənt] a.	重要的
meeting	[ˈmitɪŋ]	會議
prepare	[prɪˈpɛr]	準備
forgot	[fɚˈgɑt]	忘記（forget 的過去式）
wish	[wɪʃ]	但願；希望
worried	[ˈwɝɪd]	憂心；擔心
client	[ˈklaɪənt]	客戶
afternoon	[ˌæftɚˈnun]	下午
grocery	[ˈgrosərɪ]	雜貨；雜貨店
shopping	[ˈʃɑpɪŋ]	購物
need	[nid]	需要
plum	[plʌm]	李子
remember	[rɪˈmɛmbɚ]	記得
soon	[sun]	很快地
luck	[lʌk]	運氣
good luck		祝好運
tonight	[təˈnaɪt]	今晚

shopping	['ʃapɪŋ]	購物
pleasure	['plɛʒɚ]	榮幸
miss	[mɪs] v.	想念
sometimes	['sʌm'taɪmz]	有時
together	[tə'gɛðɚ]	一起
kid	[kɪd]	小孩子
fun	[fʌn]	好玩；樂趣
next	[nɛkst]	下一個
hair	[hɛr]	頭髮
bet	[bɛt] v.	打賭
haircut	['hɛr,kʌt]	剪頭髮
again	[ə'gen]	再度；又
grow	[gro]	留長
bathing suit		浴袍
pair	[pɛr]	一雙
shoes	[ʃuz]	鞋子
problem	['prabləm]	問題
dress	[drɛs]	洋裝
anyway	['ɛnɪwe]	無論如何
crazy	['krezɪ] a.	瘋狂的
mess	[mɛs]	亂七八糟；一團糟
huge	[hjudʒ]	廣大的
project	['pradʒɛkt]	學校研究作業
almost	['ɔl,most] adv.	幾乎

due	[dju]	到期；期限截止
halfway	['hæfwe]	到一半
yet	[jɛt] adv.	尚未
depend	[dɪ'pɛnd] v.	視～而定
new	[nju]	新的
paint	[pent] n.	水彩
paint	[pent] v.	繪畫
art	[ɑrt]	藝術
bored	[bord]	無聊的
busy	['bɪzɪ]	忙的
while	[hwaɪl]	一段時間
busy	['bɪzɪ]	忙的
work	[wɝk] v.	工作
myself	[maɪ'sɛlf]	我自己
late	[let] a.	很晚
boss	[bɔs] n.	主管；老闆
mind	[maɪnd] v.	介意
spend	[spɛnd] v.	花（時間）
fast	[fæst]	快
kid	[kɪd]	小孩子
always	['ɔlwez]	總是
special	['spɛʃəl] a.	特別
actually	['æktʃʊəlɪ] adv.	實際上；事實上
stuff	[stʌf] n.	物品；東西
easy	['izɪ] a.	容易的；簡單的

cook	[kʊk] v.	烹調；煮
frozen	[ˈfrozn̩]	冷凍的
dinner	[ˈdɪnɚ]	晚餐；正餐
on sale		拍賣
really	[ˈriəlɪ]	真的
price	[praɪs]	價格
microwave	[ˈmaɪkrəˌwev]	微波爐
ready	[ˈrɛdɪ]	準備好
aisle	[aɪl]	（貨架的）行列
watch	[wɑtʃ]	觀看
movie	[ˈmuvɪ]	電影
homework	[ˈhomˈwɝk]	家庭作業
almost	[ˈɔlˌmost] adv.	幾乎
problem	[ˈprɑbləm]	問題
left	[lɛft]	左方的；剩下的
guess	[gɛs]	猜想
help	[hɛlp]	幫助
try	[traɪ]	嘗試
talk	[tɔk]	說話
quiet	[ˈkwaɪət]	安靜的
during	[ˈdjʊrɪŋ] prep.	在～的期間
promise	[ˈprɑmɪs]	保證；答應
enjoy	[ɪnˈdʒɔɪ]	享受
shopping	[ˈʃɑpɪŋ]	購物
together	[təˈgɛðɚ]	一起

Saturday	[ˈsætɚde]	星期六
call	[kɔl]	打電話
next time		下一次
happen	[ˈhæpən]	發生
meeting	[ˈmitɪŋ]	會議
bad	[bæd]	不好
client	[ˈklaɪənt]	客戶
commit	[kəˈmɪt] v.	承諾
change	[tʃendʒ]	改變；變更
demand	[dɪˈmænd] n.	要求
satisfy	[ˈsætɪsfaɪ] v.	滿意
seem	[sim]	似乎
try	[traɪ]	嘗試
worry	[ˈwɝɪ] v.	憂慮；擔心
soon	[sun]	很快地
right	[raɪt]	右邊的；對的
finish	[ˈfɪnɪʃ]	完成
account	[əˈkaʊnt] n.	帳戶
end	[ɛnd]	結束
week	[wik]	星期
kid	[kɪd]	小孩子
go to bed		上床睡覺
already	[ɔlˈrɛdɪ] adv.	已經
doubt	[daʊt] v.	懷疑
asleep	[əˈslip] a.	睡著的

peek	[pik]	偷瞧
still	[stɪl] adv.	仍然
awake	[əˈwek]	醒著
downstairs	[ˈdaʊnˈstɛrz]	樓下的
while	[hwaɪl]	當…的時候
heat	[hit] v.	加熱
dinner	[ˈdɪnɚ]	晚餐
report card		成績單
really	[ˈriəlɪ]	真的
proud	[praʊd]	感到驕傲
smart	[smɑrt]	聰明的
mean	[min]	意思是
always	[ˈɔlwez]	總是
celebrate	[ˈsɛləˌbret]	慶祝
tonight	[təˈnaɪt]	今晚
library	[ˈlaɪˌbrɛrɪ] n.	圖書館
meet	[mit]	見面
due	[dju]	到期；期限截止
tough	[tʌf]	（口語）艱難
anywhere	[ˈɛnɪhwɛr]	任何地方；多少有點進展
understand	[ˌʌndɚˈstænd]	瞭解；明白
invite	[ɪnˈvaɪt]	邀請
discuss	[dɪˈskʌs] v.	討論；商量
sure	[ʃʊr] a.	的確的；確定；毫無疑問的
of course		當然

國家圖書館出版品預行編目資料

可以馬上學會的超強英語會話課 / 張瑪麗 · Lily Thomas一合著. -- 新北市：哈福企業有限公司, 2021.12
面； 公分. -- (英語系列；75)
ISBN 978-626-95048-7-9(平裝附光碟片)

1.英語 2.會話

805.188

英語系列：75

書名 / **可以馬上學會的超強英語會話課**
作者 / 張瑪麗 · Lily Thomas 一合著
出版單位 / 哈福企業有限公司
責任編輯 / Judy Wu
封面設計 / Lin Lin House
內文排版 / Co Co
出版者 / 哈福企業有限公司
地址 / 新北市板橋區五權街 16 號 1 樓

電話／ (02) 2808-4587
傳真／ (02) 2808-6545
郵政劃撥／ 31598840
戶名／哈福企業有限公司
出版日期／ 2021 年 12 月
定價／ NT$ 330 元 (附 MP3)
港幣定價／ 110 元 (附 MP3)

全球華文國際市場總代理／采舍國際有限公司
地址／新北市中和區中山路 2 段 366 巷 10 號 3 樓
電話／ (02) 8245-8786 傳真／ (02) 8245-8718
網址／ www.silkbook.com 新絲路華文網

香港澳門總經銷／和平圖書有限公司
地址／香港柴灣嘉業街 12 號百樂門大廈 17 樓
電話／ (852) 2804-6687 傳真／ (852) 2804-6409

email ／ welike8686@Gmail.com
網址／ Haa-net.com
facebook ／ Haa-net 哈福網路商城

電子書格式：PDF

哈福

哈福

哈福

哈福